GOOD
LOVE LUVŁ

A NOVEL

ASHLEY McCARTHY

AMP

Good Love, Bad Love

ISBN: Print edition – 978-1-8384121-2-8
       Digital edition – 978-1-8384121-3-5

Published by:

A^P
ASHLEY McCARTHY
PUBLISHING

www.ashley-mccarthy.com

Typesetting and Production: Catherine Williams, Chapter One Book Production
Cover Design: Andrew Newman Design

Printed in the United Kingdom

ONE

Nothing in this world makes your entire life flash in front of your eyes faster than watching your fiancé fucking another woman.

It's even worse when you've given up so much of your life to become a part of his. Your job, your hobbies, every bit of yourself that made you interesting. Like putty, you moulded yourself around him, becoming the wife he wanted, only to find out that he never planned to stick with that "forsaking all others" clause in the marriage vows.

It's funny how things can change so quickly. On November 12th, exactly six months prior to our wedding, I was on cloud nine. Who wouldn't be? I was engaged to *the* Piers Worthington, a man whose name sent shivers through the London banking world. Handsome, distinguished, ambitious, he was what any single woman would call a fantastic catch.

I'd just returned home from delivering a casserole to my grieving dad, being the good daughter I am. Though my visits to him usually stretched on for hours, that day, I'd been gone from the house no more than thirty minutes. "Just dropping it off!" I'd insisted. "No trouble at all!" My father had hugged and thanked me and asked

1

TWO

"If I had to come back here to live, would you let me?"

That was the question I posed to my father the following morning, as we sat around the kitchen table. The Hanukkah candles had been taken down in preparation for the Christmas boughs and trees which would be taking their place next week. The house seemed empty. We'd passed a quiet night like I loved, reading and catching up on old times. He likely put my melancholy mood down to grief, thinking of Mum and the festivities we'd had in the house over the years. He showed me pictures he'd got from my big brother Alex, who was on holiday with a few of his friends in Spain, and he'd played his Chopin CDs, which always filled me with a sense of childhood safety, since my mum never stayed long in a room without playing one.

But that question brought our pleasant visit to a grinding halt. And, as expected, I'd stricken him speechless. His mouth made all sorts of shapes, but no words came out.

My mother wouldn't have had this problem. She'd have said, "certainly" right off the bat, and never questioned it. She always knew what to say. She was my biggest fan. My champion. She gave me my courage, and she always knew what to say.

But all that crashed down in February.

My mother had been coming home from her daily walk when she'd been knocked down by a hit-and-run driver. An accident, the driver had said. He hadn't seen her. The driver, who'd had a clean record up until then and never got into a spot of trouble before, was given a suspended sentence and banned from driving for three years. His life went on.

Ours had stopped.

My parents doted on Alex and me. They gave us everything we needed and most of what we wanted. A lot of it was at the gentle urging of my mum, because she always seemed to know what that was, even before we did. She was the glue, holding our family together. So, when she was ripped from our lives, it felt like the centre patch of a quilt had been pulled out by the seams. My father, who never was the communicative sort, seemed to retreat into himself, and Alex left and devoted himself to his career, so he was no help.

A month after her death, I went to the house after a two-day absence to find my father in the exact same place; in his bed, unwashed, unfed and face swollen with tears. He was clutching a picture of my mum. That's when I decided something had to be done.

It soon became clear that my job at *Slip,* the fashion and lifestyle magazine, was going to have to go. I hated that idea—I adored that job, the work, the weekly pay cheque, the daily jaunts downtown, lunching and trading ideas with all kinds of different people. But Piers convinced me it was the best thing for my sanity. He said I couldn't keep on as my father's rock, all the while balancing wedding planning and a full-time job.

For my sanity. It was only when I looked back on it, I realised how twisted that was. Piers cared *nothing* about my sanity.

Clearly.

But back then, as much as I loved writing about the London arts scene for the magazine, and as successful as I was at it, when Piers suggested that we didn't need my income to survive, I agreed. It made sense. My father needed me. And there was always my trust fund.

A shame, really. My mother had been friends with the managing editor at *Slip,* and she'd helped me secure the placement. I soon became a part of *Slip,* a valuable part. It had been like a second family to me. The week after I left, people were calling me constantly, for my input, or to chat. But gradually, those calls stopped coming.

And then I stopped being Frankie Benowitz. I was Piers Worthington's fiancée.

That was all.

How did that happen? I couldn't be sure. I'd met Piers young, when it was a novelty to have someone of the opposite sex notice me. He was the athletic, tanned captain of the university rugby team, whom all the girls drooled over. I have to admit, I did, too. Back then, I wasn't the quiet, mousy type who let men push me around, either. I was ambitious, political, opinionated, ready to take the editorial world by storm with my words. My professors would read my work and say, "This girl's going places. Just watch." When Piers asked me out the first time, and even the second, I'd simply shrugged and said, "I'll think about it."

The third time, I'd agreed, because I couldn't resist that movie-star smile of his and because my friends said I was crazy to pass up the opportunity. Little did I know, it'd change the entire trajectory of my life.

But Piers was everything I wanted—supportive to a fault. I was prone to wildness—doing rash things like visiting clubs south of the river and driving with my petrol tank near empty. He gave me advice I thought was designed to keep me safe and secure. He cared for me, always looking out for my best interests. *My* best interests. Or so I thought.

The more time I spent with Piers, the more I started to see his mission. His banking career was his number one focus—far more important than my pursuits. Why? I couldn't be sure. It's only on reflection that I can see the undoings of myself.

Now I looked back on it, I saw that everything he'd done for me, that I'd thought was *for* me? Had actually been in *his* best interest.

Finally, something did slip out from my father's mouth, breaking the silence of the vast kitchen of the Hampstead mansion I grew up in. "Of course. But why?"

I avoided his eyes. "Oh, well. Piers and I are going through a bit of a rough patch."

He considered this. "You know," my father said gently, clearly uncomfortable. "Whatever Piers did, maybe it's not so bad. Maybe you can talk it out?"

My father wasn't the best at relationship advice. I imagine he and mum had started dating while they were still in their mothers' respective wombs. And mum was a perfect angel. He didn't know how vicious things could get between ordinary men and women. But mum had liked Piers, thought he was "good for me". So, I knew dad was speaking with her in mind.

"Maybe," I said, sipping my tea. Of course, I couldn't tell him what had happened because I was too ashamed. But I knew something had to change.

And as much as I didn't want to, I had to take control.

I tried to change the subject, casually looking around at the furnishings of the vast gourmet kitchen—the subway tile backsplash and sprigs of eucalyptus everywhere. It still smelled of lemon, exactly the way my mother had left it, but something about them seemed off now she was no longer here. "Does the housekeeper still come in? It looks a little dingy around here."

He shrugged. At one point, my parents had employed several people to keep this old home running, but gradually my father had sacked them all. Mum liked the company of the housekeeper, gardener and cook, considering them not her employees but her friends. She liked the hustle and bustle of many different bodies in the house. Their stories, their lives, always interested her, and she loved hearing from people of all walks of life—she'd said once that was what made her a great writer. I was the same. But my father was a loner. "I don't need any of that. I'm minding things pretty well, considering."

"You should still have someone come in and make you meals. I will always bring you food, dad, but you can't live on my lasagne forever."

"I don't need anyone looking after me, love. I'm quite capable."

"Right." I flashed back to the time I'd found him slicing tulip bulbs thinking they were shallots.

My phone buzzed. I looked down at a text from Piers: *You coming home soon, babe?*

He didn't miss me. He probably needed someone to get him more milk or to cook him dinner. I typed in, *Be there soon.*

A moment later, he returned with: *Do you want to pick up Chinese on the way? I'm craving General Tso.*

Of course. He was probably ravenous after entertaining what's-her-name in my absence. Or maybe it wasn't her. Who knew how many lovers he had? I typed in, *Sure,* and pushed away from the table. "I've got to go. Piers needs me."

My father was slower at rising to join me. He was only fifty-five, and yet these past few months had aged him significantly. I knew he wanted to ask more but didn't know how. Instead, we walked silently across the house to the massive foyer, with its grand chandelier, now dusty with cobwebs. He hugged me at the door, and he looked at me with kind eyes, rimmed with deep lines of worry. I hated that I'd been the one to cause them. "Don't worry so much about me. I know you have enough on your plate with Piers."

He had no idea. But Piers should have been able to do normal things, like collect Chinese food, himself. He was the one who'd chosen to add on extracurriculars that complicated his life, complicating mine in the process. At that moment, I felt a pang of guilt for having to choose Piers over the man who'd given me everything in life. *Mum would say life is a series of choices. You've made a bad one, Frankie. Now you have to live with it.* "I'll always worry about you, Dad. Please, call if you need me."

On the walk back home, I called China Palace and ordered General Tso for him, and, since I wasn't a fan of Chinese, a tub of wonton soup for me. I picked it up and arrived just as the sun was setting, wondering what surprises the house would hold for me today.

But Piers was there, on the front porch in his tech shirt and shorts, stretching. He had the thickest of hair that you couldn't help wanting to run your hands through, and a strong face with eyes that were permanently narrowed like a young Clint Eastwood, giving him the alluring appearance of someone who was up to no good. The first glimpse sent my heart skipping; *too handsome,* is what I'd always thought he was, the kind of man that didn't belong in regular society but hiding from the paparazzi. People often stopped on the street to gaze at him. It sounds crazy, but it's true. Like the sky being blue or the grass being green, it was a fact of life, something he'd likely been told since birth. He was, undeniably, breath-taking. Sometimes I hated myself for being so shallow that I'd succumbed to it, ignoring the clues that he wasn't as perfect a person as his facade would've suggested.

A bead of sweat had trickled down his temple and the trail of it glistened on his tanned skin. "Good timing. I'm famished."

He went to take the cartons from my hands and leaned in for a kiss. I stiffened. So entranced was he by that night's dinner, he didn't notice as his stubble grazed the side of my cheek.

I said, "We need to talk."

He was already heading inside. "Can we talk while we eat?"

I supposed I had no other choice. I had absolutely no appetite, but I followed him anyway, always one step behind him, like his tail. I watched him from the kitchen doorway, pouring a healthy helping of rice onto his plate, and covering it with the chicken mixture. "We have any soy sauce?"

I winced. I'd meant to buy more, at the shop this week. "I don't think so."

"*Damn.* You need to start making a list, so you don't keep forgetting things."

Again, I winced, wounded, until I remembered: I had bigger things on my mind.

Watching him shovelling it into his mouth, I finally summoned the courage. "Who was that woman the other night?"

His eyes snapped to mine. I knew the inevitable next words would be him professing his innocence, saying *What woman? I have absolutely no idea what you're talking about!* so I beat him to the punch:

"I saw you. In bed with her. I was standing in the doorway. You didn't see me."

Piers was always good at concealing his emotions. It came with being a dealmaker; that poker face was what usually made the person on the other side of the table agree to anything he said. His chewing slowed, and he swallowed with some difficulty, but otherwise, there was nothing. Finally, he said, "Adrianna. From accounts payable."

I waited for an explanation, an apology, a profession of, *but it's you I love!* Any of those things would've made this situation better.

Nothing came.

Finally, I said, "Do you love her?"

His answer was immediate, so immediate I didn't trust it, not like I'd ever trust anything he said again. "No."

"You said you did."

He let out a short, ironic laugh. "So? I *said* it. I didn't mean it."

He said it so casually, I had to wonder what else he'd said that he didn't mean. My salmon *en croute* probably wasn't that phenomenal, after all. He was so eerily calm, it jarred me. He was about to *lose me.* Didn't he get that? Or did he not care?

He set the plate down and came over to me, but I flinched away.

He stopped, clearly annoyed that I was so hurt by this. As if I were overreacting? "Look. Frankie. Yes. I have sex with other women. But I'm marrying *you*. That has to say something to you, doesn't it?"

I could only stare at him. *Women.* As in, more than one. And nowhere in that declaration did he mention that he intended to *stop* sleeping with those women. There was no remorse in his declaration. No, "Sorry I did it." Not even a "Sorry you caught me."

So yes, he was right. It *did* say something to me. It said I'd been a huge mug.

"You need to stop."

He recoiled as if slapped. I know, it must've been a shock. Since when did the lowly Frankie Benowitz ever demand that Piers Worthington do anything? The corner of his mouth seemed to rise into a snarl, which became a kind of sick smile. "Believe me, Frankie. You wouldn't like me if I stopped. Is that what you want? Me, coming after you, three times a day? Maybe more? Because I will. Trust me, babe. This arrangement is best for all of us. In fact, I'm glad you know about it. It was exhausting, keeping it from you."

I stood there, letting his words sink in, hearing the tinny drip-drip-drip of the faucet, alternating with the clock, ticking on the wall. He didn't intend to stop. In fact, with it out in the open, maybe instances would increase. Maybe I'd be expected to invite them in, cook them my possibly phenomenal salmon *en croute* for sustenance while they fucked upstairs.

Jessica's voice came to me: *Kick him in the balls.*

"The wedding is off," I said, my voice hollow.

For a moment, it was almost like he hadn't heard. Then he snorted and pushed away from the counter, grabbing his food, and scooping it with a fork. "Don't be daft, Frankie. You can't do that. Your father put down all that money on the banquet hall. Stop with the hysterical drama."

"It's off," I insisted, surer this time.

He simply nodded slightly and looked down at his plate. "Fine. It's off. You wanna go, go. We'll see how that works out for you," he said, shoving the forkful of chicken into his mouth.

I stared at him, waiting for the penny to drop. For him to realise what he was losing and beg me to stay.

That didn't happen. Instead, he swallowed and said, "Look at you. You're not the woman I proposed to. Ever since your mum died, you've let yourself go. It's sad. So, I'm glad. This is for the best."

I'd wanted to wound him. But he certainly didn't *look* like he'd been kicked in the balls. In fact, he looked perfectly fine. Too fine; less upset than when I'd told him there was no soy sauce.

And just like that, I wasn't Frankie Benowitz, feature writer at *Slip.* I wasn't Piers Worthington's fiancée.

I was absolutely nothing.

THREE

I stared in the free-standing Louis XVI antique mirror in my childhood bedroom and sighed.

My dress was black and elegant, with a wide boat neck that exposed my clavicle, stopping just above the knee, with long sleeves and an open back. I'd bought it for some cocktail party Piers wanted to take me to, knowing that bankers always dressed like they were going to a dress-up funeral, and as a rule, their significant others followed suit. In my year-long engagement to Piers, I'd learned the rules of that world, little good they did me now. The dress felt like a war wound; an unpleasant, lasting memory of a past life.

I smoothed the fabric down over my curves. Where once, the dress was figure-hugging, now, it sagged in places, especially at the chest. Why were my boobs the first thing to go? I'd lost weight, the result of having no appetite whatsoever. Despite loads of make-up, my eyes were still sunken, my face drawn. I looked as if I'd recently emerged from a long illness.

I placed my hands over my stomach. I may have lost weight, but I'd always had a bit of a spare tyre there. If we had been on the normal timeline, the timeline where I'd be marrying Piers, I'd be getting ready for my first dress fitting. Piers had said, too, that he wanted kids "as soon as possible". I touched my stomach, imagining a baby growing there. Piers' baby. In an alternate universe, that could've been my life.

And maybe I'd be happy.

Well, happier than now.

Now, nearly two months after the breakup, I was no better than I'd been the day after. At first, I'd told myself it would take time. Dr Hargrove had said that, too— "Give yourself the time you need to grieve!" I'd been gentle with myself. I'd holed up in my bedroom, popped Ativan at will, and waited for the grief to pass, for the motivation to move on. But as time went by, and none of that happened, I got more and more depressed. What if Piers was truly the best thing that ever happened to me? Maybe I was being selfish, wanting him to myself. What if I'd cut off my nose to spite my face and now there was a glaring hole there, one that would *never* go away?

My father usually left me alone to wallow in my bedroom. And I did. I kept the shades drawn, and the covers pulled up over my head, for most of the day. I'd even spent most of the Christmas period staring at the Yule Log programme on the television and remembering the way Piers had dropped to one knee in front of our Christmas tree, a year ago. My family had all been there. The guests cheered and congratulated us, and champagne flowed like water. And at the time, I'd considered it the highlight of my life, with so much more to come.

Now, I had nothing to look forward to. Not one thing.

So, when my father nudged me out of bed earlier that morning, it was as much a shock as an earthquake. "What? No," I'd said, trying to burrow deeper.

"I've had this New Year's Eve party every year since before you were born, love," he said. "I'm not going to give up the tradition on your account."

That was when it struck me. My father's parties were legendary. His law firm, Benowitz Partners, was one of the most prestigious in London. And the guest list read like a who's who of London society. Of course, he would have it this year. There had been rumours that he wouldn't be able to continue at the helm, and the party said as much about the health of Benowitz Partners as it did about him.

And if he could do it, so could I.

I slipped on my mother's teardrop earrings and stared at myself in the mirror. Not much of an improvement. I wrapped a long red pashmina around my shoulders, one my father had brought me from New York. The tassels danced around my waist.

Piers would insist I wear my hair up, I thought as I fingered a string of my long dark hair. Something about me looking too young for my age. The smattering of freckles over the bridge of my nose didn't help. He said when I coiled my hair in a chignon, it helped me to fit the part.

Fuck it.

I pulled the band out of my hair and let it fall loose on my shoulders. Better.

Then I stepped out the door, into the hallway.

Downstairs was already hustling with servers, decorators and chefs. Christmas music was playing, and sprigs of holly adorned with white fairy lights and red velvet ribbon were everywhere, including on the railings of the sweeping staircase to the gleaming white marble foyer. We may have been Jewish, but that didn't stop the Benowitz family from pulling out all the stops for the season.

I peered over the rail, past the enormous crystal chandelier, to see waiters, buzzing around like honeybees tending to their hive, putting in the last-minute touches. As I did, the grandfather clock downstairs began to chime nine o'clock, and the first doorbell rang.

Party time.

Taking a deep breath, I went downstairs as a servant opened the door, blowing a gust of icy air into the fire-lit entrance hall. Guests began to arrive, shaking snow from their coats as they handed them off and accepted glasses of champagne and *hors d'oeuvres*. Some, I recognised; most, I didn't. Instead, I grabbed a flute of champagne merely to keep my hands busy and meandered toward the two-story Christmas tree which stood proud in its usual spot by the staircase.

I tried not to think of the way I'd shook like a leaf as Piers slid the ring on my finger, just over a year ago, on this very spot. I'd looked over at my mother, who was beaming, eyes wet. I felt a pang in my heart, and tears threatened to spill from my eyes. Back then, I thought it would be the two of us, Piers and me, a team, forever after. Now, it was just me against the world.

"Hey, sis."

I turned to the familiar voice of my brother Alex, standing there, looking very dapper indeed in his tuxedo. "Oh!" I leaned in to kiss him, feeling so much better and less alone. Funny how we'd fought like cat and dog as kids, then eventually drifted apart. Now, I was so happy to see his familiar face. "Hi." We embraced in a tight, loving hug. "You bring anyone?"

He dug his hands into his pockets and smirked. "Nope. You get me to yourself."

"Lucky me," I said, peering behind him because I wasn't sure I believed it. Alex was the life of every room he entered. He didn't go places alone. "You sure you didn't bring any of your friends along?"

One of his dark eyebrows arched significantly higher than the other. With that look, in that tux, he could pass for a gentleman. "Oh, I see. You want me to fix you up?"

Growing up, it was all I ever did—tag along after his friends, the little sister who lingered outside his bedroom when his mates were around. I annoyed Alex intensely. But engaging beyond an ego-boosting flirt with eligible men was the last thing I wanted to do now. "Nope. Done with that."

His smile fell. "I'm glad you called it quits on him, Frankie. Really. If he was going to—" He stopped and, at that moment, I realised he must've known about the woman. There had to have been gossip. And he was a social magnet, drawing everyone to him, so there wasn't much he didn't know in the London scene.

I cringed. I hated being part of gossip. I'd safely avoided it, most of my life. Now, I'd be at the centre of it. "He wasn't always the best boyfriend. But I did think he was loyal. I was wrong."

"Maybe. But you know, Mum never liked him."

My gaze flashed to his. "What? You're wrong. In fact, a year ago, she stood right here and cried when Piers proposed. Or did you forget?"

"Frankie. Maybe that was because her baby was growing up?"

I stared, open-mouthed. "How did you—"

"She told me. She worried about you. She thought Piers was entirely too absorbed in himself and said she hoped you weren't making a mistake."

I couldn't process this. "She never told me," I murmured, but of course, she wouldn't. She wanted for me whatever I wanted. And I'd wanted Piers. I had a momentary thought of her, so worried about me on her walk home from the shop, that distracted, she'd stepped out in front of—

No. I needed another Ativan. But they were locked in my room. I settled for a gulp of champagne, instead.

"Well, Piers was kind of a—"

"I don't want to talk about it, Alex," I said with a sharp intake of breath. "Can we just enjoy the party?"

His voice was quiet. "Sure."

We turned toward the doors. More people had arrived and were mingling in tight circles. Something was missing, but it only took me a moment to realise what.

My mother would be wearing bright red, dancing among them, tossing about holiday greetings and witty banter, the *belle* of the ball. She'd flutter from group to group like the charming social butterfly she was. She'd put everyone right at home.

"I love you, sis," came out of the silence between Alex and me.

Although I hadn't heard him say this since we were kids, I smiled and squeezed his hand as we scanned the growing party. "I love you too, A."

Alex let out a breath and downed his glass of champagne. "This place looks like a mortuary. Better get out there and host," he said, setting his flute down and straightening his lapel as if he were about to go live on television. "How do I look?"

I smiled. "The most handsome man in the room."

He rolled his eyes and started for the buzz of the forming party, mumbling under his breath, "I miss Mum."

I stood there, alone, knowing I should help with the hosting duties, but somehow rooted to the spot. I drained my glass and took another from a passing server, knowing I was well on my way to tipsy. Fine. I could totter off to some dark area of the garden outside and wallow in my depression and no one would even notice; I could even treat myself to a good cry.

I'd just made the plan to do so when I looked across the room and noticed Michael. My breath hitched and my mouth went dry. I'd always thought he was handsome. I'd harboured an all-consuming crush on him as a child, with his waves of dark hair and strong, movie-star jaw. But now, in that tuxedo, he looked even more so. Our living room was suitable for the upper crust of society, but he seemed even too beautiful to be standing in it.

Michael was an associate at my father's firm. He'd been a friend of the family for years though, and had attended school with us. He and Alex had been friends—not the best of friends, though. More like the type that were thrown together out of sheer boredom whenever the adults got together and threw their dinner parties.

He was standing at the fireplace, staring at the large portrait on the mantle of my parents, me, and Alex. It was outrageously pretentious and silly—we were positioned like stiff royals, unsmiling, standing a few inches apart from each other, as if we couldn't bear to be near one another. Every time I went into the room, I cursed that painting.

But Michael was eyeing it like it held all the secrets of the Universe. Tall and slim, he leaned toward it, circling the rim of his champagne flute with one finger. *What on earth in that ugly monstrosity has him so entranced?* At first, I thought he was inspecting the name of the painter, which had been scrawled on the corner, right over my foot. But then his eyes lifted slightly, and I wasn't sure … I didn't want to indulge such a thought, but the more I stood there, the more it fastened in my mind … was he looking at … me?

When he turned and noticed me staring, his dark eyes lit up. He made his way over, weaving through the crowds.

"Miss Benowitz." He offered his hand, like this was a business deal. I shook it, noticing the contrast of his deep olive skin with my own. His hand was smooth and large, mine practically got lost in it.

"Mr Evans," I said, matching his tone. "Or you *could* cut the formalities and call me Frankie, Michael."

He smiled. "All right, Frankie." He said it in a stilted way as if testing it out. He had a deep timbre that echoed pleasantly in my ears. No one had ever said my name like that before, it was nice.

"Did you have a good Christmas?"

"I did. I spent it in Dubai. You?"

I spent it under the covers. "It was … nice. Quiet. You know."

"Uh," he said, and I knew what was coming. Michael was a brilliant attorney. He didn't get tongue-tied. I braced myself for it. "I suppose I should offer my regrets at the end of your engagement?"

I shrugged. "Why? I don't regret it. Not in the least. *I'm* the one who ended it. I wonder if the rumours mention that?"

He frowned. "I don't—I only heard that it had ended. Not the particulars."

Maybe he was saying it to be nice, but I immediately felt shitty for my curt answer and assumption he'd been one of those gossipmongers who were always poised, champing at the bit for news of anyone's misfortune. Michael wasn't like that. I didn't know him well, but my gut had always told me he was one of the good guys. After all, my father often groused about the associates he worked with but never had a bad word to say about Michael.

I quickly changed the subject. "So, you were in Dubai? My father actually gave you time off of work for the holidays?"

He appraised me for a moment, in mock shock. "Now, Miss Benowitz. Your father isn't a slave-driver."

I laughed. "Frankie," I corrected, because I wanted to hear him say it again. "So, what's in Dubai?"

He shrugged. "Warmth," he said as if that was all the reason in the world.

"Yes, I suppose, but what made you go there?" I asked, sure there was a girlfriend at the other end of this. Piers dragged me to exotic locales for holidays all the time, rather than endure having to sit around a stuffy dinner table with blue-haired relatives, discussing the same inane things again and again. Really, though, I liked the idea of a holiday at home. Snow. Family gathered around. A roaring fire. Hot chocolate. This time of year, was the only time I didn't mind the cold.

"Just wanted to get away. Really disconnect from everyone and everything."

"Everyone … You mean you went alone?" I must've looked horrified because he laughed.

"Yes. It's actually not as torturous as it seems. I happen to like my own company. And it gave me the chance to think."

I wish I could have come with you. It was on the tip of my tongue, but I was afraid I was being too intrusive.

After all, in all the years I'd known him, this was the most I'd ever talked to him without Alex there. Instead, I said, "You're a free spirit."

He'd been sipping his champagne, but he stopped abruptly and swallowed. "Why do you say that?"

"Anyone who'd go on holiday on their own is—"

"Well, maybe your father drove me to it." He laughed, and I noticed when he smiled that he had one dimple on the side of his cheek. Just one. I'd heard that with faces, the more symmetrical they were, the more attractive they appeared. But that wasn't the case with Michael. The asymmetry suited him; his face was filled with warmth, compared to the self-love I'd always seen in Piers' face, over the years.

"But you like your job. You must. My father's always talking about how good you are. 'Michael this,' and 'Michael that.' You're clearly one of his favourites."

He shrugged. "I do like it. Most of it. Some parts, not so much. But on the whole, it's good. Pays the bills. I couldn't imagine working in a job I didn't love. You can't show passion for something you don't *feel* passionate about."

He was being humble. I wasn't exaggerating when I said that about my father. My father rarely spoke about work without saying how incredible an attorney Michael was. "A young me," he'd called him, once. "You make people very comfortable," I observed. "You're easy to talk to."

When it was out, I blushed. That was awkward. Why had I said that?

37

"Part of the job." He smiled sheepishly, either sensing my embarrassment or not comfortable with having attention aimed at him. "How are you doing with your writing?"

I smiled. "How did you know—"

"Your father was always talking about *you*, to *me*. All the pieces you wrote. He has your first one, framed, in his office. Are you back at the magazine?"

My stomach sank. I'd considered going back, but I kept finding excuses not to. I had no motivation. Deep down, I didn't know if I could write like I once did. With most people, I was ashamed to answer the truth. Many times, over the past few weeks, I'd brushed the question aside, winding around the topic before swerving onto another one. But for some reason, I felt comfortable answering. "No. I stopped that earlier in the year after my mother died. My father needed me, and ... well—"

"Your dad looks like he's doing much better. You think you might start up again?"

"Oh. Uh ... yes. Maybe? I'll probably start looking after the holid—"

"There you are! Look at the mole, she's finally peeked out of her little cave!" Jessica's loud voice rang through the living room, making everyone turn. She had a champagne cocktail in each hand, looking vibrant in a bright green dress like she'd just walked off the runway. She leaned over and kissed my cheek.

"Moles live in holes, not caves," I teased.

Not that Jessica paid any mind to that titbit of animal education. "You're wanted on the dance floor."

"By—"

"Me, of course!"

"Oh. Okay," I said, glancing at Michael. I wanted to keep talking to him.

She downed one of her glasses, set it aside, and grabbed my hand. Then she winked seductively at Michael. "You, too, tall, dark and sexy."

Spurred on by champagne courage, I grabbed his hand, and we weaved our way, like a train, through the crowd, to the ballroom. There, a DJ in a Santa hat, and sunglasses was playing old-school hip hop music that reminded me of my uni days. People were getting into it, too. The mixed age groups, ranging from retirees to teenagers, were jumping up and down on the dance floor as if it were a rave.

"My father has made some strong choices for this year's party", I said with a chuckle. It felt alien to laugh.

The truth was that last year's party had been very sedate. My mother had set the tone for that, making it into one of her refined, sophisticated events. For this year, my father had said he wanted to liven things up—not because he wanted a drunken dance club in our living room, though. No, he didn't want any reminders of what things had been like *before*. And this was definitely doing the trick. I never thought I'd see the stuffy ballroom of our elegant house, a house which had once entertained members of the royal family, reduced to a frat house basement.

We started to dance—or jump was more like it. Bodies were pressed so closely together that I kept getting elbowed and nudged, but I didn't care. It felt good. Piers, had he been here, would never have approved of this; not for me anyway. There was always an excuse to keep me away from this sort of fun; I was dancing too close to some men, and they weren't to be trusted, or it wasn't dignified behaviour for his fiancé. Knowing that, I found myself smiling for the first time in ages.

"Who's the hot guy?" Jessica shouted to me over the throb of the bass as we moved, nodding subtle side-glances over to indicate Michael.

Mortified, my jaw dropped. "Shh! He can hear you!"

She laughed. "No one can hear anyone!" she bellowed.

I looked over at him. Sure enough, he continued jumping to the music, shaking a fist in the air, oblivious. Like most of the guys, he'd loosened his cravat. He was getting a bit of a five o'clock shadow, and I had to agree with Jessica: This slightly more deconstructed version of Michael was undoubtedly hot.

"You should go for him, girl!" she shouted again into my ear. She did a twirl and raised her hands up over her head, much to the delight of a few of the older lawyers around us, whose eyes were glued on her trim, statuesque figure. "No ring on either of you. Nothing's stopping you!"

"*No*," I said, looking over at him. He was one of the few guys in the vicinity who *wasn't* looking at Jessica. I'd not known him to have a partner, either. *Hmm. Maybe he was asexual?*

Still, the last thing I needed was a man. Not while I was still navigating my way through life after Piers. And Jessica knew this. She knew I'd barely ventured outside, except for my twice-weekly sessions with Hargrove. Oh, she'd invited me out plenty of times, but I always said no. She kept telling me I needed to put "distance" between myself and Piers. In her book, that meant sleeping with someone else. Maybe even several someones. Actually, in her book, the more, the better. *You need to get under someone to get over someone. Or don't fuck. Just kiss. Flirt. Date. Have fun. The more you do it, the more you'll forget about him, until he'll just be a smudge in your rear-view mirror!*

"But who are you gonna kiss at midnight then?" she asked with a grin.

Ugh. Right. I'd forgotten that horrific tradition. Well, it wasn't horrific when you had someone, and I'd had Piers, for years. It was actually fun when you had someone, like Valentine's Day. I remember looking at all of those singletons on Valentine's Day, thinking, *how sad, glad I'm not one of them.* But there was nothing sadder than having no one to kiss at midnight on New Year's Eve. I thought he'd be my New Year's kiss every year, for the rest of my life.

Shoving those thoughts away, I shrugged. "Well, I was gonna smooch you, but if you're trying to tell me you don't want to, I'll have to find someone more worthy of my affections!"

"Remember!" she shouted. "*Distance!*"

Right. How could I forget? She'd told me almost every time we talked on the phone for the past few weeks.

I tried to ignore her, but she leaned in close, so close I could feel her breath, tickling my ear. "Seriously, girl.

That's your mission. If you choose to accept it. Kiss that hot guy. Make it epic. So epic, Piers is nothing more than a bad memory! Okay?" She shot a couple of finger guns at me to press her point and backed away to mingle with the crowd.

• • •

An hour later, Jessica's mission was all I could think about.

I was on my umpteenth glass of champagne, so I was in the strange, weightless place between tipsy and blacked-out. If I *had* popped an Ativan, I'd have likely been comatose. Drinking this much on an empty stomach would lead to regret the next day, but I told myself, with drunken seriousness, *that was future Frankie's problem, not mine!* I'd drank so much simply because of the mission at hand.

At that moment, I was hell-bent on succeeding. I stalked about, take-no-prisoners style, wavering a bit in my drunkenness, intent on capturing Michael's lips.

At one point, a bunch of us went outside to the garden, where the slightly crumbling fountain stood central in the courtyard. There was Jessica, Michael, and Alex. There was also a guy who looked like a ferret, with weird, beady eyes, who seemed infatuated with Jessica. His name was Stephen, maybe. And there were a few other girls who Jessica knew from uni, who may or may not have been sisters or even triplets, since they kind of looked alike. It was just as crowded out there, so even though it was chilly and damp, it wasn't so bad. Soft music was being piped in from invisible speakers, scattered around the garden. We were drinking and dancing and laughing and waiting for the New Year.

At one point, one of the triplets, who was clearly drunk, took off her shoes and went into the partially frozen, shallow water of the raised fountain. We watched this with amusement, as she tried to dare some of the boys to go in with her, splashing playfully at them. Finally, Alex sat on the edge and started to pull off his dress shoes.

I leaned over to Michael. "Are you going in?"

He chuckled. "I may be sloshed, but I am still very aware I'm in the company of the boss's daughter."

Great. So, he had decorum. That probably meant he wasn't going to kiss me. I'd have to do the heavy lifting here. I gazed at his lips. They were lovely, full lips. For a moment, I imagined how they'd feel against mine. Would he kiss like Piers, hard and urgent, taking control? Or would he be softer?

Piers had kissed me during our first meeting. The first *hour*. He'd come right out at a mutual friend's party at uni, and put his lips on mine, his eyes saying, *you know you want this.*

And I had. Though I hadn't actually agreed to a date until the third time he asked me out, we'd got the kissing out of the way, early on.

I tried to convey a little of Piers' raw sexuality to Michael, that come-hither, doe-eyed look that made men want to kiss women, but it seemed lost on him. He was watching Alex, who was clearly smashed, frolicking with one of the maybe-triplets, splashing each other.

I moved away so I wouldn't get wet and took another sip of my champagne. Now, it was kind of bitter. I didn't think I could have another glass. Perhaps I'd move to water before bed.

Or perhaps not. Maybe I'd fail in my mission, remember I had nothing to live for and decide to get as sloshed as the girl in the fountain.

Michael noticed and took a step back with me. "You all right? You're not cold, are you?"

I wasn't sure if he was asking because I was the boss's daughter and it was the right thing to do, or if he cared.

Before I could say any more, he wrapped a strong arm around me.

God, it felt warm and heavy. He was wearing some manly, woodsy aftershave that I wanted to swim in. It had hints of lime, I thought, as I resisted the overwhelming urge to bury my nose in his throat. And his body was delightfully svelte and strong. He'd removed his jacket, and the muscles of his arm and chest pressed against me, solid and inviting.

I wanted to lean my head down on his shoulder. I was about to when one of the triplets looked up from her phone and shouted, "Hey! Guys! It's time."

In unison, we began to chant into the starry night. "Ten … nine—"

The excitement built. People giggled and whooped. "Eight … seven."

My heart thrummed. I took a deep breath, ran my tongue over my teeth. "Six ... five ... four—"

Swallowed. Closed my eyes and prayed I could do this. "Three ... two ... one—"

Distance. Put distance between you and Piers.

"Happy New Year!" everyone shouted at once.

I turned to Michael, ready to lay that kiss on his lips when I realised someone had beaten me to the punch.

Alex grabbed Michael by the lapels, brought him close, and gave him a big, drunken kiss on the lips.

"What the fuck, you wanker," he shouted, laughing as he wiped his mouth in disgust. "Blimey! You taste like shit!"

Alex smirked at me and pulled Michael away.

I stared, dumbstruck by my stupid brother, until Jessica came over and wrapped me in a bear hug. She kissed me full on the mouth. "Happy New Year, beautiful," she slurred, as Auld Lang Syne began to pipe through the speakers accompanied by the crowd.

"Happy New Year," I replied, my stomach twisting in absolute disappointment. For the first time, I'd wanted to put that distance between myself and Piers ... and now he never felt closer. Like I could feel him, breathing down my neck.

My father came out, looking so dashing in his tuxedo with a rather faraway drunken look on his face. He waved and gave wishes to the guests he saw, but bee-lined it toward me. He kissed me. "Happy New Year, love. Having a good time?"

I nodded, even though, right then, I wanted to go to bed. All of a sudden, the party felt like such hard work. I knew I would regret getting so pissed I couldn't even stand. I was drunk, tired, and a thunderous headache was forming between my eyes.

Everyone headed for the doors. I followed them, trying to think of what excuse to use on Jessica for ducking out early, or whether an Irish goodbye would be a better option. Headache. That was a good one. And—

I stopped suddenly when someone grabbed my hand.

I looked back to see Michael, smiling with that adorable dimple.

"Want to dance?"

I looked around. "What? Here?"

"Sure."

The old paving slabs were slick and wet from the other guests' earlier exertions in the fountain. But a slow song wafted out from the ballroom, and we had the entire patio to ourselves.

So, I let him take my hand and pull me to him. He gazed into my eyes, and he held my hand, just barely, his fingers closed around mine. I felt as though I had forgotten how to breathe as his warm hand slid down my bare back.

He gazed at my lips, but I knew, as much as he might want to, that he wouldn't try to kiss them, out of respect to my father, out of respect for me. "Happy New Year, Frankie," he murmured.

I could've leaned in and kissed him. But this moment

felt so perfect that even a kiss could ruin it. Instead, I laid my head on his chest and we swayed together, quietly, for the rest of the song.

Baby steps, I thought, and enjoyed the moment.

FOUR

Two days later, another shock came my way.

After the party, I'd been slowly pulling myself back into normality. New Year's hadn't been a complete awakening, but it had done a little something to nudge me out of my shell. I'd actually updated my CV and started looking through the online jobs market for editorial positions whilst still nursing a horrendous hangover. I'd figured I'd ease my way into the employment waters, maybe send out a few inquiries and see if I got any nibbles. Take my time.

No rush, so I thought.

I sat in the window nook of my mother's office that morning, sipping my tea, and reading a book. My mind wandered to my mother. I read here every morning because it was her office, and it made me feel close to her. She'd been a freelance writer when I was very young, and had worked from home, so I would toddle into this room, and she'd pull me on her lap and let me pound on the keyboard. When I got a little older, sometimes we'd play a game, pretending that we were in a busy newspaper office. I'd write crazy stories about ponies and dragons, knights in armour and damsels in distress. It was such fun. I smiled, looking up at the floor-to-ceiling bookcases lining the walls, and curled the blanket tighter around me as I cradled the novel in my lap.

My father came downstairs, wearing a suit; I can barely remember an instance when he wasn't either in a suit or a pyjama suit. His tie was askew, as usual. I stood up and straightened it for him.

"What would you like for din—"

"Frankie, we need to talk."

I blinked. As far as I was concerned, we *were* talking. I was going to ask him what he wanted for dinner, like I usually did, and then, after my visit with Dr Hargrove and when my father returned home, I'd have it ready for him. That was our routine now. As I mentioned, I *liked* routine.

But at that moment, I got the very distinct feeling that he was going to upset the routine.

I sunk down into the window seat, bracing myself.

"What do you mean?"

"I mean that I think I've been doing you a disservice, letting you hide away like this. Giving you time. I thought you could go at your own pace, but I never thought—" He sighed. "You know I understand what it's like to grieve. But sometimes, you need to be given that little push in order to move on. So that's what I'm doing."

"Little push?" I didn't like the sound of that. "I'm not standing still, Dad. I'm moving, maybe slowly, but—"

"Look at you," he said, shaking his head.

"What's wrong with me?" I looked down at myself.

Clearly, I was a disappointment. Sure, I hadn't showered

49

since the party. And yes, I liked slobbing around in mismatched sweats and a messy bun. But ... easing in. No rush. That was the plan.

"You need to get out there."

"Oh. I will. I have another appointment with Hargrove today."

"That's not what I mean."

I knew exactly what he meant. "I updated my resume," I explained. "And I was going to—"

"I got you a job."

I froze. "What?"

"Not a full job, but an internship. Paid. I called in a favour with a friend of a friend. It's for a magazine. So, you should fit in well," he said, looking sadly over mum's things.

I nearly bit my tongue. This was so *sudden*. "Okay, but—"

"Your passport's up-to-date, right?"

"Ye-es," I said, wondering why it mattered. "Wait. Where—"

"It's in Miami."

"Miami," I murmured the word, almost to myself, trying to think of what other Miami he could be talking about. Surely not the one clear across the Atlantic. The one that made it pretty damn impossible to turn around and come home, should I decide that this was a massive mistake. "You mean the one in the US?"

He nodded.

"Oh, but I can't! What about Dr Hargrove? We've been making such progress. And—"

"I spoke to Dr Hargrove, actually. It's all been arranged. You can call in. One of those e-conferences. Zoom." I soon realised I was a passenger rather than a participant in this conversation.

"Yes, but—what about—" I think my whole life flashed before my eyes, again. Of course, I'd been a bit of a world traveller so that didn't bother me. But this felt different. More dangerous. Like space travel. Alone in the void. In an attempt to take control of the situation I blurted out "I still have things to settle around here—"

"Like?"

Nothing came to mind. So, I pulled out my last protest, even though I knew what he'd say, which was why I was saving it in the first place. "But what about *you*? I can't just leave you!"

"I assure you, you can. I'm an adult, Frankie. And I want you to do this." His tone was firm, in a way it only got very rarely with me.

I stared at him. "Are you ... trying to get rid of me?"

"Oh, love. No. Not at all. I'm trying to *help* you."

I looked around helplessly, frantically. I'd be leaving this – my nice comfortable shell – behind. Entering a minefield. I'd wanted to slowly ease myself in. But my father wanted me to jump in head-first, without even testing the waters. This sounded dangerous.

But then again ... like Jessica had said, it was about creating distance between myself and the terrible things plaguing me in London.

Maybe this was what I needed to do. Create a lot of

distance, physical distance, and fast, like ripping off a plaster.

So, I took a deep breath, and forcing myself not to think too much about it, said, "All right. When do I leave?"

Funny how the moment the words left my lips, I thought of Michael, holding me close on the patio, outside the house, on New Year's Eve. That hadn't been so terrible.

In fact, it'd been rather nice.

FIVE

The sultry warmth hit my skin as I stepped out the sliding doors of Miami International Airport, wheeling my bags on a luggage trolley. Bright banners, emblazoned with the words "Welcome to Miami!" in pinks and turquoises, greeted me. I slipped on my dark, oversized sunglasses to guard against the blinding white sunlight and soaked it in as I checked on Saucy, my teacup Chihuahua. "How are you, little guy? Toasty here, isn't it?"

He yipped cheerfully. I smiled at him, the cutie. I'd bought him four days ago, so I wouldn't have to take this trip alone, and he was already ranking up there as one of my cleverest purchases ever. No, he wasn't a big strong man who could carry my luggage for me, but still, he made the trip into the unknown ever so much more tolerable.

While I'd never been to Miami before, I'd been to plenty of tropical, exotic wonderlands, principally in southeast Asia. The Maldives and Thailand were practically a second home to me, so when my father had mentioned Miami, I knew that the weather and I would get along fine. It certainly beat the often-dreary days of London in January.

Standing in the taxi-line, most of the other travellers

looked a bit miserable, sweat-stained and rumpled, fanning their faces with their hands, not that it did much good to ward off the oppressive humidity.

But the abundant sunshine, combined with the distance, were already working wonders on *my* mood. Balancing my tiny dog carrier, I shifted my passport and phone to my other hand and smiled from ear to ear.

Why hadn't I done this sooner? I thought, pushing up my shirt sleeves. *I'll even get a healthy glow! Piers will be jealous. He loves this weather.*

My smile faded. Fuck. I'd thought the "P" word.

I checked my phone. I'd told myself I wouldn't think of him, now I was on this side of the pond, only four minutes ago, while standing at the baggage carousel.

That's all right. You're allowed to make mistakes, I told myself as I stepped forwards in line. The driver of the next cab looked over the luggage trolley, laden with my bags, and opened the door to the cab for me. "Welcome to Miami," he mumbled half-heartedly. "You don't travel light, do you?"

I couldn't tell if he was being sarky, so I decided to give him the benefit of the doubt.

"Thank you!" I said, sliding in, the backs of my thighs sticking on the cracked and faded vinyl seat. "Yes, I'm going to be here for a while!"

The driver, an old man with white sideburns and a few stray white hairs atop his head, slipped into the seat, wiped the sweat from his neck with a handkerchief, and gazed at me through the rear-view mirror. From his brightly coloured print shirt, he looked like he should be relaxing on a beach somewhere, sipping a drink with a little umbrella, and in a *much* better mood. "Where to?"

"Four Seasons."

He gazed at my dog carrier. "Figures." He plugged something into the computer on his dash. "A Brit, huh? What brings you here? Vacation?"

"Oh, no. I'm working. I just got an internship over here," I offered too readily. *See, I'm not some spoiled trust fund baby. I'm a working, spoiled trust fund baby ... with a father who pays for everything.*

It did the trick because his voice softened. "Ah. That's a shame. But don't forget to put that bikini on. This is Miami, after all!"

I smiled as he took off, swerving us into traffic so quickly I nearly got whiplash. "Believe me. I am looking forward to the beach."

After I get this work stuff sorted through.

I shivered, despite the heat, my nerves catching up with me. The seven-hour flight out of Heathrow had been mostly uneventful. I'd had a seat in business class next to a stodgy Wall Street type who spent the entire time hunched over his laptop. It hadn't bothered me. I'd wanted to take an Ativan with my glass of champagne, to ensure I had a restful nap on the plane, but it hadn't mattered. My nerves had been so shot from the past few days' planning, Saucy and I had fallen asleep before the plane had taken off, only waking when we touched down. It was probably the most restful flight I'd ever taken.

Now, though, the jitters came back, full force. It didn't matter that my father's friend of a friend had pulled strings in my favour. In fact, that made me even more nervous. I wasn't clear on the details – my father had tons of friends – but all I knew was that I hadn't got here on my own merit. And that made me feel like I needed to impress these people, they had to know I was worthy.

Plus, Americans were different. Don't get me wrong; I loved America and I'd been to New York City countless times. I just wasn't sure they'd love me. Outside, everything in Miami looked so functional. It wasn't like England, where things were packed into a space too small for its parts. People milled around on the streets at a leisurely pace, soaking up the sun—no, it wasn't like cold, dreary England at all, where everyone hustled to get out of the weather, and the damp crept into your bones for nine months of the year. As I looked out at the people among the plentiful palm trees whizzing by, I wondered if I'd be *too* different to work for them. They liked confidence, and I, well, I lost that a long time ago and had no idea how to get it back.

I pulled out my phone to find a text from Jessica: *Miss you already.*

Smiling, I sent a text to her and my father that I had landed, then pocketed my phone and tilted my face to the sun. The windows were open, and the fresh sea air blew through my hair. I pushed it from my face as the cab drove onto Route 1 towards downtown, the road overlooking the beach. The sand was gleaming white, the water a pristine blue. I caught glimpses of it between the skyscrapers as the cab slowly navigated its way through traffic.

"First time here, huh?" the driver said.

Embarrassed, I realised I was hanging off the edge of the seat, my head nearly out the window like an excited Labrador. It didn't matter how much I'd travelled; I couldn't help but be enthralled by the sights of a new destination. I was always a tourist, eager to experience and learn. My parents took me everywhere as a child, and I stayed in the most illustrious, five-star resorts. I wasn't sure why my stomach was churning with such an odd mix of excitement and fear.

Maybe because for the first time, it was just me. Alone.

"First time to Miami, yes."

"Well. Once you put on that bikini, you'll fit right in."

I shifted uncomfortably, because men didn't usually talk to me like that, and he'd mentioned a bikini twice now. Usually, I was with *him,* and people knew better than to talk about me donning a bikini around him. I didn't own one, partly because I wasn't very confident about my body – I was all limbs with a spare tyre – but also because I knew he'd hate men ogling me. Not that they did. Or at least, I never noticed such things. But he was always telling me to cover up, that I was making a spectacle of myself.

I should buy a bikini, first thing. Just because.

I swallowed as the cab pulled under an overhang outside a skyscraper made entirely of mirrored panels. A couple of valets jumped forward, eager to help, and opened the door for me. "Welcome to the Four Seasons," an attractively scruffy, tanned man in a red jacket said to me. "Checking in?"

"That's right."

He and his partner started to load my bags onto the luggage cart. "Right through those doors. We'll take care of your bags, ma'am."

"Thank you." I rummaged in my purse for my credit card and swiped it, wondering what to tip. This was America, after all. I never had to handle tips when I came to New York. That was always up to someone else. My parents, or P—*him*. I cleared my throat. "I'm sorry, what's the customary tip?"

The driver looked at me like I'd sprouted another head. "That's up to you, ma'am."

In the stagnant, humid air, I'd begun to sweat, even out of the direct sunlight, beneath the overhang and a canopy of thick palm fronds. He'd had all those bags to deal with, so I pressed the button for twenty per cent, hoping I hadn't made a terrible faux pas.

"Thank you."

I peeled my sweaty thighs off the seat and stood up, then slammed the door behind me and headed for the revolving door. I pulled off my sunglasses as I stepped into the sparse, modern lobby, adorned by palm trees and a gurgling fountain. Sunlight streamed through the many windows as my heels clicked on the granite floor on the way to the reception desk.

"Good morning," the woman behind the desk said with a bright smile. She was wearing a blazer adorned with a golden placard that said her name, *Violet*. "Checking in?"

I nodded. "The name's Benowitz."

"One moment." She tapped into her computer. "Francesca Benowitz. I have you staying in a suite for a period of two months?"

"To start. Yes, that's right," I said, hoping my father's secretary had made the arrangements correctly. As she continued to type, I leaned against the counter, wondering if any famous Americans had been here. Donald Trump? Taylor Swift? Or maybe Mel Brooks. Was he still alive? My father and I loved his films, and we would always watch them together when I was growing up.

The clerk handed me a key card and gave me directions to the elevators. "Top floor! You'll need to use the key card in the elevator to have access. If there's anything you need, Miss Benowitz, anything at all, call us at any time," she said.

I collected the key with an awkward smile and headed for the bank of elevators. When the doors opened at the top floor, I looked around the place and sighed.

My father said it would be good for me to have this nudge out of my shell, but this was far from tough love. The place was massive, a huge corner suite, and full of cream walls and white furnishings. The outer walls were floor-to-ceiling windows, one side overlooked the hotel's rectangular pool while from another I could view a strip of the glaring white beach. It was like living on a cloud. Only the best for his daughter.

Thanks, Dad. Now, to settle in.

I yawned.

I don't want to settle in. What I want to do is lie in the warm sun and sleep, like a dog, with no real responsibilities at all.

Letting Saucy out of the carrier, I went to the phone and called the front desk and asked if they'd send up some tea. When they told me they would, I hung up and walked to one of the windows and stared down at the many people, like ants from this distance, walking along the shoreline, playing in the blue waves. Then I went to the massive king size bed and flopped back on it.

I didn't get jetlag now, but as a child I suffered terribly on planes. In fact, when I was five or six, my family and I took a trip to Thailand. Then, I'd vomited almost twelve hours straight, from the moment the plane took off right through to our destination. I'd puked all over an older gentleman's Panama hat, and he'd been none-too-pleased. Luckily, hundreds of trips later, I'd become accustomed to travel. My rules: travel business class; sleep the whole way and miss everything you're paying for; always bring toothpaste and a washcloth to use before landing and dress comfortably; make sure you take a neck pillow and warm thick socks, eye mask and good quality ear plugs, then stay up until bedtime in your new time zone after a big, carb-free meal.

I yawned again at the thought. It was still morning, and already, I could've done with a nap. But I needed to stay up, so I could be bright-eyed and bushy-tailed for tomorrow, my first day in the office.

Dread fell over me anew, but I pushed that thought away. *No sense worrying about it now. Worry tomorrow, future Frankie can deal with that.*

Startling me from my thoughts, Saucy yipped, wanting to be up where I was, so I leaned over, scooped him up, and set him down beside me.

"What do you think? Nice, huh?"

He'd already got lost among the pillow pile at the head of the bed. I laughed at his little legs pinwheeling up and over, as he rolled off the cushions and onto the turned-down duvet. He looked up at me with what I like to believe was love and a little embarrassment. Piers never wanted us to have a pet. He said he was allergic, but he disliked *anything* small and cute. In his mind, it meant weakness. Looking back, I think it probably had more to do with my attention being taken away from him.

Shit, Frankie. You're doing it again. I was beginning to get annoyed at how my thoughts still drifted to him all the time. It had been two months since I'd caught him in my bed with his *sexcretary.*

I scooped Saucy out from the pillows and said, "What are you gonna miss?" as I cradled him against my chest. "Yeah, you're right. We won't miss anything, will we? Hmm, Dad? Yes. We'll miss Dad. And maybe Alex."

He started to bark loudly, just as someone rapped on the door. "Bell services."

I sprang up. "My luggage!" My clothes felt damp with sweat. I couldn't wait to change out of this baggy top, into something light and linen. I'd dressed in comfortable warm clothes upon leaving England and changed on the plane into shorts and zip-up top; but even this was too warm. *It'll take a few days to acclimatise.*

I opened the door to find the bellboy from downstairs, as well as a woman in a black dress and apron. The placard on her chest said *Karla*. "Does madam need help with her unpacking?" the woman said in fractured English.

That was probably too much if I was going to go about my father's mission of proving my independence and resiliency, but as I gazed at my luggage, a sense of inertia washed over me. "Yes. That's great. Thanks."

The bellboy wheeled the cart into the bedroom and went out, leaving me alone with the woman, who efficiently set about opening my suitcases and taking out the items, placing them in the chest of drawers.

"Most of the items in that bag," I told her, pointing, "should be hung up."

She grunted. Meanwhile, I watched her, wondering which of my suits I should wear for my first day on the job. Or should I wear a suit? Maybe it was better, in this kind of climate, to dress in slacks and a light blouse. Yes, probably.

Karla was very good at keeping everything straight. She unpacked with almost machine-like precision, folding everything with extreme neatness. I watched her carefully. "Thank you for helping me to unpack. I can never do it in an organised way."

The woman actually smiled, until Saucy barked at her. "Why you visit here? With your dog!" She seemed half amused, half baffled.

"I took on a new position. At a magazine," I said, glancing outside. I had no idea where anything in this town was. "Do you know where there's a shop—I mean, a store, where I can buy dog food?"

She pulled out a bright pink sundress, shaking away the creases, and placed it on a hanger. "There is a Publix around the corner. Ten-minute walk."

"Oh. Thanks," I said, filing that away for later as I pulled my cosmetic case out of the big suitcase and placed it on the vanity. "So, how long have you been in Miami?"

She gave me a questioning look. I got the feeling I'd surprised her; maybe I was the first person to ever ask her a personal question. "Ten years," she said quietly.

"I like to hear about people. Their stories. I'm a writer," I explained. "Have you always worked in this hotel?"

She nodded. "I usually work laundry, but they were short-staffed in housekeeping. I do not think I will stay much longer. The people in this hotel act like animals. Oh, the sheets—" She shook her head as she slammed the last drawer closed and flipped the lid on the suitcase. "Terrible! I'll move these to the closet."

She started to move them into the walk-in closet, as I went through my purse, trying to figure out what kind of tip would be reasonable. Shit, was I supposed to tip the bellboy? Probably. No wonder he'd been staring at me.

When I turned around, she was standing there, waiting for it. I took a rolled twenty and laid it in her hand, then tittered. "It's funny. You never think of who is washing your sheets."

The second it was out, I cringed. I hadn't meant it to sound rude, but the woman snatched the money away and glared at me like I was a world-class, snobby arsehole. "I guess your sort doesn't," she snapped, spinning on her heel.

I was still cringing, long after she left. Not in Miami for an hour, and I'd already stepped in it. My only hope was that tomorrow, my first day in the office, I wouldn't do it again.

SIX

The following morning, I felt like that six-year-old me in Thailand.

Oh, I'd got plenty of rest, so I knew it wasn't jet lag. It didn't stop me from hanging over the toilet, puking my guts out, twenty minutes before I was due at 1200 Biscayne Blvd, the headquarters for *Miami Scene, the Magic City's Premier Entertainment and Lifestyle Publication*. My nerves were prickling like crazy, and I felt hot and feverish, like I was going to pass out.

Half-ready to call Gillian, my new superior, and tell her I needed a sick day before I'd even started, all I could see was my father, shaking his head in disappointment. Somehow, I don't know how, I wrenched myself up from the bathroom floor, brushed my teeth, grabbed my brief-case—which housed a sad-looking apple and my phone charger—and headed out.

After taking Saucy to doggy day-care, I arrived at the office on the fourth floor of a modern skyscraper, miraculously, with five minutes to spare. I tried to keep my exterior as composed as possible while my insides churned like a slushy machine, and the ice-cold aircon helped keep any more vomit from rising in my throat. I walked into a vast waiting room with a large reception desk. Again, everything here was sparse—the only *décor* were various covers of the magazine from over the years and a few tropical vibrant green plants which contrasted the white walls.

I winced as I approached the reception desk and realised, I'd never even *seen* a copy of *Miami Scene* before, let alone researched it. It was probably pretty important for their new writer to know a bit about the magazine they're about to write for. *What was I thinking?* I couldn't believe I'd made such a rookie mistake! It was unlike me to be so unprofessional, but my mind had been a fog for the past couple of months. Trying to find the old Frankie in that mist was a challenge that I had to start facing.

As I was freaking out, one of the four headset-wearing receptionists finished her call and looked up at me. "Can I help you?"

I glanced along the line. They were not just pretty, but *gorgeous*—slim, tanned, and suitable for magazine covers. Each one had a head of stick-straight hair in various shades, from black to blonde. They were so perfect; they were practically animatronic. "Uh, hello. I'm Francesca Benowitz?"

I'd hoped that would be all the introduction I needed, that she'd say, *Ah yes. The new intern.* But she continued to stare blankly.

"I'm here to see Gillian Conway."

Her eyes narrowed. "Is she expecting you?"

I nodded. *I hope so. Otherwise, this'll be a long trip for nothing.*

She dialled the extension and spoke quietly into her mouthpiece as I tried to pretend I wasn't listening. "Yes, Gillian. Sorry to bother you."

You can learn a lot about the management simply from the way the administrative staff interacts with them. My supervisor at *Slip,* Carole, one of my mother's best friends, was a true gentlewoman, a woman even the lowliest intern felt at home with. But, *Sorry to bother you?* With a simple phone call, informing her of an arranged appointment? Things were not looking good for Gillian Conway. Was she a total nightmare? God, I hoped not, my fractured nerves felt ready to smash at any given moment.

"Someone's here for you. A—" The receptionist continued, eyeing me from my head to where my chest disappeared beneath the massive reception desk. "What did you say your name was?"

"Francesca. I go by Frankie."

"Francesca," she spoke into the mouthpiece. "All right. I will." The call ended without so much as a *Goodbye.* She motioned to some sleek but awfully uncomfortable-looking red metal chairs in a corner. "Have a seat. She'll be with you in a moment."

"Thanks," I said with a wavering smile.

I wandered over and was just about to seat myself when the double doors opened and a forty-something woman with a severe face of botox bordered by a blonde bob came blustering out, hand extended. "Francesca?" she said, smiling wide. "How wonderful to meet you! I have heard so much about you! I'm Gillian."

I shook her hand. Maybe my first impression was totally wrong, but her American enthusiasm replaced my nervous anxiety with bludgeoning jitters. "Frankie, actually."

"Frankie! I love it!" she gushed. "Come on back. Super accent, by the way. We do love our friends across the pond!"

I followed her back, feeling slightly better knowing I'd been expected. I must've been, because she led me to an empty cubicle that already had a placard with my name on it. It wasn't anything too impressive, white walls and rather drab, industrial-grade grey carpeting, but it was larger than mine at *Slip*.

"This is your home away from home," she said, presenting it to me with great flourish. "Set your things down and I'll introduce you around to our team."

I smiled and put my things on the task chair, noting how, despite the beautiful blue skies outside, all the cubicles and workstations seemed to be situated in the centre of the drab floor, as far away from the windows as possible. *Was that on purpose?* My cubicle at *Slip* had been tiny, but it had a great big picture window, overlooking St James's Square.

I suppose it made sense; it was easy to get distracted by Miami. Not in the place for ten minutes, and I already wanted to gaze out at the lovely white sand beaches.

Gillian was wearing a sleeveless shell and black slacks, just like me. She was as chic as any of the younger receptionists outside, and far more confident. Everything she said was punctuated with an exclamation mark, signalling a zest for life that seemed impossible to fake.

"This way!" she said, leading me to an open area, where three young men and two women swivelled around on their chairs to stare at me. "This is our design team! Everyone, this is Frankie, our new editorial intern! She's from London!"

She introduced me to them, and I tried to be cheerful and smile a lot, but everything said went in one ear, and out the other. I was never very good with names. I tried to make myself repeat each name thrice upon meeting, but the whole thing went so quickly I knew I wouldn't remember my own name by the end of the introductions. After that, she took me to the sales department, where I met several older ladies, and the editorial department, where I met a couple of stoic young men with too much facial hair who didn't seem to want to be bothered. In the end, I met over thirty employees in a variety of roles, not one of whom had a name that stuck with me.

Oh, except Dane, one of the previously mentioned editorial guys who didn't want to be bothered, but was, predictably, *ridiculously* handsome. He had a goatee, and his hair looked like someone had run two hands through it, mussing it up. All I could think was, *Now, if you wanted a full one-eighty from Piers, there he is.* Piers went everywhere with a comb in his pocket, and he shaved religiously. The one thing they had in common. Good looks. From his swagger, I could tell that he, too, was told often how beautiful he was.

Dane, however, like most men of his type, utterly ignored me, except for a grunt and half-wave tossed vaguely in my direction.

Finally, Gillian led me back to my little cubicle. She sat me down, turned on the computer, and showed me how to find my email. Then she checked her gold watch and said, "Well, I have to go. I have a meeting. You'll be required to meet with HR this afternoon, but right now, I'll send Tori over. She's our admin. She'll show you how to work our project management software. So happy to have you on our team!"

I smiled. "Happy to be here!"

Gillian left, her heels clicking fast as she walked purposefully away. I picked up my phone to try to set up my voicemail, but before I could, a tiny pixie with girlish, corkscrew curls flew into my cubicle and hoisted her left buttock cheek onto my desk.

"Hey. I'm Tori."

The girl couldn't have been more than twenty. She was wearing an impossibly short skirt and impossibly high platform heels, and she had a tattoo of a sun on her inner wrist. "Hi, I'm—"

"Frankie, I know. You're British. You're our new intern." She leaned in and whispered, in a very conspiratorial way, "Welcome to hell."

I nearly burst out laughing. She had to have been exaggerating, the place seemed great so far. I'd had a couple of dramatic friends who were like that—they saw the worst in every situation. Maybe Tori was like that.

I *hoped* she was like that. I didn't need any more stress in my life right then. "What do you mean?"

She smiled slyly. "It's hard to recognise Satan, I've heard, but guess what? You just met her!"

Talk about maddening. Now I knew *Miami Scene's* admin was wrong. Because how could that smiling, perfectly sweet woman be so bad? "Gillian? She seemed pretty nice to me."

"Nope. She's not."

I leaned back in my chair. "You're joking."

She crossed a finger over her heart and held up a hand in oath. "I promise I'm not. I've—"

She stopped and straightened, hearing something, then looked up over the cubicle wall. The next time she spoke, she was quieter. "Trust me. We can go for drinks later and talk more. Or ... do you British just do tea?"

I couldn't help but giggle at the sincerity in her face. "I do drinks," I said, excited about the invitation, my first social engagement in Miami. All the same, I wasn't sure I wanted to be friends with someone who was so clearly ready to relay the worst about people to strangers. That could be dangerous, but I had resolved to assimilate here before my plane had left Heathrow—throw myself into professional and social life. The only way to do so was to give everyone a fair chance.

"Good. Tonight?"

I nodded.

"All right. Let me show you this thing," she muttered, jiggling my computer mouse, and leaning forward. "It's so easy, any idiot could do it. You're going to be logging the articles in here, shifting them from department to department when they end up in your inbox, and marking when you've received the final version."

I frowned. "That's it?"

"Yeah. That's the intern's job. Why? Did you think you'd be doing something else?"

"Well, I'm a writer. I've written hundreds of pieces for the previous magazine I worked for. I was thinking I might be working on some—"

Her eyes were wide with revulsion. "The intern? Not a chance. Seriously. She, Dane, and Gabe are the only staff writers. Everything else is freelancers."

"Oh," I said. Well, my father hadn't done *everything* for me. This was good. I needed a challenge. I'd have to find a way to get my work in front of her. Not a problem. I could do that. Gillian seemed nice enough, how hard could it be?

Although the perky thundercloud Tori made it seem downright impossible.

"Trust me. You'll be hating life here, by the end of the week," she said in a sing-song voice. "If you manage to last that long."

SEVEN

Tori had lived in Miami all her life, so despite being the harbinger of doom when it came to *Miami Scene,* she was the perfect person to help me get settled in. Only a local could help me do that. I would find out the best places to eat, shop and sunbathe. And I desperately needed to make friends on this side of the Atlantic, if only to let my father know that I was capable of surviving on my own.

And I needed to prove that to *myself,* too.

So what if the job wasn't exactly what I'd hoped for? It was something to do, something different from my old life. The essential duties were taking notes, fetching coffee, and pushing paper from one person to the next. I didn't think I'd show up as intern on day one, wow them with my prose, and be promoted to *Miami Scene* feature writer by close of business, but I'd at least thought it might afford me some upward mobility, an opportunity to claim what I'd once had at *Slip.* But from down at the very bottom of the hill, I could barely see the summit.

After Tori finished showing me how to work the photocopier and helped me upload an attractive avatar to my profile on the project management tool, I spent a good deal of time stapling packets to go inside the *Miami Scene* media kits. I paused for lunch only long enough to get a bag of pretzels from the vending machine, and then it was back to stapling. By five o'clock, my fingers were as damaged as my pride.

So, when Tori arrived at my cubicle, jingling her keys, and said, "I think we should go to the Art Deco district, to give you a taste of the real Miami," I was putty in her hands.

We drove in her 'bug'—a little red convertible, to the section of South Beach I'd only seen in old movies. The buildings were the typical explosion of washed-out pastel colours with sleek curves and polished chrome. It was love at first sight, my feelings ebbing away from anxiety and into excitement at this new and thrilling place. Everything shone in the late-day sun, which was still so hot and bright, I was glad to have my sunglasses. If this was Miami mid-winter, I could imagine me making a home here for good.

We went to a place called The Flamingo and sat at a table on the sidewalk, under a beach umbrella. I ordered a champagne mojito because it sounded very Miami. Tori asked for chips with extra salt and salsa, then slipped off her cardigan and pointed across the street. "That's Muscle Beach over there."

I glanced at a couple of men, lifting weights on the sand.

Tori, however, licked her lips. "Yum. Look at that one."

No thanks. To humour her, though, I glanced at a muscle-bound, hard-chested man. His torso was a rug of brown hair, cut through by a tight Speedo. "Nice," I said, trying to feign enthusiasm.

"What's the story with you? Are you married?" She dipped her sunglasses, her eyes fastening on my bare finger. "No?"

"Nope! Single as can be!" I somehow managed brightness. I didn't want to go there. Not yet, especially with a girl I'd just met, so I quickly changed the subject. "So, tell me about Gillian. Is she really that bad?"

"Worse. I've known her for two years since I graduated from college and got the job. I'm twenty-four now, and I swear, she's the most aggravating person I've ever met!"

I eyed Tori. That meant she was only two years my junior, despite the youthful appearance. It had to have been the corkscrew curls. "If she's so terrible, how have you managed to last?"

She laughed. "Because I'm a little insane. I guess I like the punishment. Besides, I need the money. I have a bit of a spending problem." She pointed to her Versace purse. "But Gillian's terrible. She'll rip your heart out and stomp on it, and then make you think everything that went wrong is your fault. She'll take credit for your good ideas then slit your throat and leave you dangling if you—"

"Sounds like my ex!" That popped out before I could even stop myself. I might not have been able to stop myself from thinking about Piers, but I thought I'd at least be able to stop myself from *talking* about him. I tried to be sympathetic, but she was scaring me with these claims. Now, I hoped she was exaggerating. "But she can't be that much of a nightmare."

"Oh, she is."

"She has to have some good qualities?" I prompted.

Tori pretended to think and then shook her head. "I can't think of anything. All the other supervisors in the office give their people gifts and half a day off for Christmas Eve. She gave us a telling off and made us work late."

I winced. I'd heard American holiday time wasn't good. At *Slip,* I'd got five weeks of holiday, so I took a month off every summer. I figured I'd be needing whatever time I could get if only to go back and visit my dad. "How much vacation do we get?"

"Five days to start."

I paled. "*A year?*"

"No sick time for your first ninety days, either so don't plan on coughing up a lung on us. She won't be sympathetic in the least." She took a sip of her margarita. "But please. Don't let me scare you all the way back to England. Why did you leave there, anyway? Something to do with that ex?"

"It's a bit of a long, sad story, I'm afraid," I said.

She leaned in close, hands framing her delicate oval face, her eagerness unmistakable.

I laughed. Maybe I was the eager one, desperate to fit in and find a friend on this side of the Atlantic or Tori was simply someone I felt comfortable with. Anyway, I told her everything. All about Piers, how we met, dated, fell in love, and got engaged. Then, of course, since I'd had two mojitos and rather loose lips, I told her about what happened afterward. She gasped at the appropriate times, which made me feel better, and wrung her hands in outrage.

"That jerk. How could he do that to you?"

I shrugged. "I don't know. It's fine. It's been a while. I'm over it." At least, I wanted to be.

She shook her head. "Well, it's a good thing you came here, then. Miami has the best-looking guys in the country." Her brow wrinkled. "You're not dating anyone else, are you?"

I laughed. "I haven't had a chance to meet anyone else!" Then, of course, a thought of Michael flew into my head, as it usually did when I wanted to remind myself that life wasn't all bad. The way he'd held me on that dance floor was quickly becoming something I clung to, like a security blanket. "Well, there was one guy, Michael. But he's all the way on the other side of the ocean, now."

"Okay. Anyone here?"

"I just got in yesterday! So, the only men I've met so far have been the bell boys at my hotel, and some of the people at the office, Gabe and Dane and—"

Her face scrunched in disgust. "Oh, trust me. You don't want to go there."

"Trust me, I wouldn't dream of it!" I laughed more. "The last thing I want to do is crap in my own nest or get involved with men right now."

"Good. Because well, Gabe's gay, so there's that." She said with disappointment, "But Dane? He's so full of himself, it's ridiculous. You saw him, right? He probably didn't say two words to you?"

"Right! At least I know it wasn't just me."

"Definitely not you. He's like that with every woman.

He's such an ego. Hot, brooding, but a total ego. Oh, and I saw him at a club once, making out with three different girls over the course of a night. I think he'll fuck anything that moves."

My nose scrunched. That sounded like *you-know-who*.

She leaned back and her eyes darted towards the sidewalk, which was a lot busier, now the sun had set. Neon lights were shining all over the strip, and the air seemed to sizzle, not just from the heat but from the energy within it. Women with a lot of make-up and not a lot of clothes, and men with gold chains and open-collared shirts prowled about. Latin music played from invisible speakers. Everyone seemed to be in a partying mood.

Tori grabbed a chip and started to nibble on it. "So, do you think you'll be back at the office tomorrow?"

I smiled. "You haven't scared me away yet."

"Face it. The whole stapling job was probably worse than Chinese water torture. And I can't promise you the work's going to get much more exciting, unfortunately."

"Do you *want* me to quit?"

"No! You're the first normal person they've brought in. The last person smelled like corn chips, kept a picture of her ferret on her desk in a wedding frame, and almost attacked me with a staple remover."

"You're serious?" I was getting the impression that Tori had a penchant to exaggerate, but I didn't mind this. Jessica was also prone to hyperbole. I thought it best to take what Tori said with a pinch of salt and get to know her better. I was starting to like her as the early evening wore on. Even if she was a little OTT, she seemed good fun to be around.

She nodded. "So, you're a breath of fresh air. I'm sorry if I'm unloading on you. I don't have anyone else to talk to about it. The admin staff are the lepers of the building, in case you didn't realise."

I polished off the rest of my mojito, feeling it warm my tummy. "You make the job seem so delightful. I don't know why you don't have people lined up around the corner."

"Sorry," she said again. "It's just so easy to complain about that place. Did you really think you were going to be able to write for the magazine?"

"Well, I wrote for a culture magazine in London. *Slip.*"

Her eyes widened. "I've heard of them. Why did you leave?"

"Because my mother passed away suddenly and Piers thought it'd be a good idea for me to concentrate on family. Plus, he didn't want me to work when we were married."

Her jaw dropped in indignation. "Bastard."

"But when our engagement ended, the job, unfortunately, wasn't available anymore. Besides, I wanted to get away. When this job came up, I thought it would be a good opportunity," I said, leaving out the part about my father getting me the job. "And it's fine if I'm not writing. I could probably stand to expand my skill set. Even if that is just stapling, for now," I said, noticing the mojito had given everything I looked at a fuzzy hue. Wow, that must have been a strong drink.

"Well, I'm glad you're here. It sucks, yes. But you and I are going to have so much fun together. I can feel it."

When we finished, Tori dropped me at doggy day-care where I collected a very happy but very exhausted Saucy. My plan to walk back to the hotel didn't sit well with him, so I ended up carrying him most of the way home. We went upstairs, both tired, but feeling happy. I'd accomplished something. Something big. I'd stepped outside my comfort zone, done something stressful and scary, and I'd succeeded.

Yes, Tori said the job was terrible. But I couldn't help thinking that good things would come from it. The connection with her was a good one, and only the beginning of the great things that were going to happen to me. I could feel it, too.

But then I had the misfortune of looking at my phone as the lift climbed to the penthouse. There was one message, from Jessica: *Have I got the guy for you!*

EIGHT

"Drinks tonight?"

I looked up from yanking a staple misfire from the stack I was trying to collate to find Tori peering over the cubicle wall at me.

"Drinks?" *Hadn't we done that LAST night?*

She nodded. "I sure could use it."

I sighed. I could've, too, at that moment. Maybe Tori was a budding alcoholic, but ever since Jessica had messaged me, I'd been feeling the pressure of the impending date.

Jessica worked in her family business with her mother and was an interior designer for the rich and famous, so she travelled the world, fixing up homes. Last night, we'd texted well into the midnight hour, about some man whose home she'd done in Miami. Eric something-or-other, who was handsome and clearly rich, since he'd afforded Jessica's services. He was recently divorced, she'd said, and out on the hunt. She knew nothing else about him, and yet seemed convinced that it was a match made in heaven.

When I told her I wasn't sure, she'd texted back, *Come on, take a risk!*

Sure. Jessica took risks as easily as she breathed. Which was probably why she was living the life of her dreams.

Career, money, happiness … she had it all, doing exactly what she wanted to do.

Serendipity, she'd texted. *Of all the towns in the world, you two are in the same one! I gave him your name and number and he's going to call you.*

He hadn't called, yet, but the previous night, looking at women in slinky outfits on the South Beach strip, I decided that I was woefully under-prepared for any date, should one arise. Thanks to Piers' "modesty is everything" credo, my outfits made me look like a Puritan, living in the pre-indoor-plumbing ages.

So I'd made the decision to go shopping.

"I have other plans. Do you know of any good department stores?"

Tori's eyes blazed with a new kind of fire. "That's like asking if a fish knows of any good oceans. There's a mall right down the street, or we could drive out to Sawgrass Mills, it's *the best* place to go shopping in Florida. We can go after we get off. Why?"

I didn't mind her inviting herself along. In fact, I was happy I'd have the company. "My best friend's setting me up on a blind date."

"Oooh, a blind date? Do tell!" She slipped her butt up onto the desk again, waiting for the juicy details.

I didn't have any. "Just some guy. I don't know anything about him. But I don't have any good date clothes, so I need to get out there."

She rubbed her hands together greedily. "What's your budget?" she asked, her eyes widening. "Well, girl." she continued before I could answer, "Leave that to me. Forget the mall. I know precisely where to take you."

I trusted Tori because for the past two days, she'd dressed well, in cute skirts and blouses, which were professional yet didn't make her look like an old schoolmarm. Her skirts were a bit on the short side for my liking, and she bared more cleavage than I was comfortable with, but I figured I'd be able to find something wherever she shopped.

We wound up going to Worth Avenue and meandering through designer and boutique shops. The streets were immaculate and, like everywhere else in Florida, lined with beautiful palm trees. As the daylight started to fade, pretty white fairy lights were turned on; hanging in waves between the trees. My mind wandered and Michael was with me, walking along the cobbled lanes that jutted from the sides of the main shopping avenue.

"That. That's the perfect dress for a blind date," Tori's words brought me back to reality. We gazed into the window of a trendy shop. "And it'll look amazing on you."

I looked up to see a pretty, blush-pink slip dress on a mannequin. "You think that would look good on me?"

It was completely not my style, but – of course – I meant it was not Piers' style. I'd been with him so long that I wasn't even sure I had my own style anymore. Maybe this pink number was it? It looked short, but still stylish, with spaghetti straps, hanging loose on the small mannequin. Had Piers been here, it would have been a no. He'd probably have admired it on any woman who wasn't attached to him, but for me? He would have looked at it with a mildly disgusted expression, which would've made me lose interest. Sometimes, when shopping, I'd have to predict what he wouldn't like about an item of clothing, so when he'd prompt me to disapprove of it with a "What do you think of this?" I could spit back to him everything he was thinking. If my assessment didn't totally agree with his thoughts, I could usually expect a patronising speech about why I was wrong.

But he wasn't here, now.

"You won't know for sure until you try it on!" she said, hooking an arm through mine and dragging me into the store. She ordered the sales clerk to take it down from the window, and shoved me into a dressing room with it. As she did, she glanced at the price tag and grimaced. "Or … not."

The sale price of $800 didn't worry me. I had the money now that I was away from Piers. I didn't think about dropping twice this amount on a day dress back home. So if it made me feel confident *why not?* I smiled and picked up the dress.

"If you can afford to drop that amount on a dress, then why are you an intern for a sadist?"

"We all have to work, Tori. Besides, it keeps me out of trouble"

I had bigger things on my mind. Like, when was the last time I'd been on a date? Five years ago? What was the dating world like, these days? I had no idea. The world seemed a lot more frightening than my pre-Piers days. What if this man was a serial killer, and I ended up his victim?

I put the hanger on the back of the door and stared at the dress, this completely un-Frankie dress, trying to summon the courage to put it on.

"You can do this," I whispered out loud as I stripped to my bra and knickers.

Then I picked up the dress and threw it on. It got stuck, likely because I was missing something. A hidden zip, somewhere.

Spinning around blindly, trying to shove it down over my shoulders while searching for the zip pull, I groaned as something tore at my hair. "Jessica! This is all your fault!" I grumbled.

On the other side of the curtain, Tori said, "You okay, Frankie?"

"Oh, fine!" I said blithely, my face red because I could barely breathe through the fabric. I finally located the zip and yanked on it, freeing the dress from its tight tangle around my shoulders, and pulled it down.

But it still stayed in a bunch around my boobs. I felt like a sausage, being stuffed into too little casing. I tried to smooth it down over my backside, but the fabric had no stretch whatsoever.

Who am I kidding? I mumbled, looking at myself. I wasn't just half-dressed and in slight pain. I was certain I wouldn't be able to get *out* of it now I'd got partially into it.

Kneeling on the floor, I reached around my back and managed to peel the thing off. As I did, I heard a slight rip and felt one of the seams giving way. I winced, hoping no one outside heard that. Then I looked at the tag.

Size 0.

Ah ha! So that was doomed to failure, from the start. I spun around and looked at my saggy rear. Awful. It was no one's fault but my own that I'd stopped going to the gym, the second the wedding got called off.

I put it on the hanger and threw it over the curtain rod. "This one appears to have a massive rip in it," I said innocently.

Tori didn't buy it. "Oh! Let me see if I can find you another."

"No, that's all—" I stopped when I heard her heels, clicking away from me. "Can I get a 4" I called out louder.

I stood there, half-naked, looking at my pasty skin in the fluorescent light, repeating, *What am I doing?* over and over again in my head. I'd put physical distance between me and Piers, but maybe now I needed to work on the emotional.

At that moment, I thought about Michael. Dancing with him, under the stars, at New Year, had done wonders for my confidence. Now, every time I got a little nervous, I went back to that moment, that moment when I'd felt human again, able to make a connection, however fleeting, with another person. My skin flushed at that thought. *Yes, wherever possible, I should try to make more of those moments.*

Another dress flew over the curtain, startling me from my thoughts. This one looked bigger. I took it and eagerly slipped it on.

"Better?" Tori called.

I tilted my head and swished the skirt. It showed skin. A lot of skin. More than I was used to. But I liked the feeling, and it was far from indecent. In fact, it enhanced my curves in just the right way, with its tight bodice and flowing skirt that hit a good few inches above the knee.

Bracing myself, I pulled back the curtain and offered myself up for inspection from Tori and the rest of the women in the shop.

Tori took one look and clapped her hands. "Girl. That is *it*."

Sold.

"But can you ... eight-hundred dollars?" She winced.

"It's not a problem," I said, spinning in the mirror. As I did, I saw Tori's mouth go wide. I'm sure she was wondering exactly what kind of intern goes shopping for eight-hundred-dollar dresses she'll probably only wear once.

I smiled, feeling good about the date for the first time. Maybe, just maybe, I wouldn't make an absolute fool of myself.

• • •

Saucy was waiting for me in our hotel room. I'd decided to leave him at home today due to how tired he was at the end of each day. He jumped up to greet me and gave me big puppy kisses. I gathered him in my arms and checked my phone. I had a text.

Frankie. This is Eric, Jessica's friend. Are you up for drinks tomorrow? Say eight at The Cuban?

I stared at the message. So, was that how dating went these days? A text? Why risk giving too much about oneself away, appearing too human, with a phone call? I wondered if it was possible to delete the message and pretend I never received it, then go on with my life.

No, Jessica wouldn't let that go.

But really—asking a woman out via text? It seemed like a lazy move.

I quickly rang Jessica. A sleepy voice answered. "Hello?"

"Oh, shit. What time is it there? Well, it doesn't matter. Listen to me. I—"

"It's one in the morning, here, Frankie. Thanks very much."

Knowing Jessica, she probably hadn't been asleep long. I thought one was before her bedtime. I took a deep breath. "I have to tell you this. I don't think I can do this."

"Do what?"

"The date. With Eric. I don't think I'm ready. How well do you know him, again?"

"Oh!" Now she sounded wide awake. "I don't know him at all, really. But he's hot, has a nice flat, and didn't say anything too offensive—that I can remember. There were also no human heads in his freezer, which is a big plus. Did he call you?"

"No. He texted."

"Texted? Hmm."

"That's a wanker move, isn't it?"

"Well, not necessarily—he could have been busy at work or something. I told you. He's rolling."

"So am I." I collapsed on the sofa. "I don't need this stress. I don't need a man. I need another Ativan."

I opened the amber bottle and looked inside. I only had three left. I hadn't yet been in touch with Hargrove to start our Zoom sessions, but I needed to do that. She wouldn't prescribe for me unless I was seeing her. And … where would I even collect the prescription? My nerves started to zing again.

"Look, darling. Fortune favours the brave. Confidence is a confidence trick. The enemy is your inner-me. And all that tripe," she said in her no-nonsense, plummy voice that instantly brought a smile to my lips.

Still, I wasn't Jessica. Far from it.

"That's easy for you to say. You have bags of confidence. I just have bags under my eyes and arse."

"Frankie, for the last time, stop," she said in her husky voice, sounding like a stern schoolmaster, scolding a child. "You need this. The guy might be a wanker, yes, it'd be good if he is, then you'll get the chance to say, *I don't want this.* And the more you say no to guys, the easier it'll get. There is nothing more liberating than saying no to a guy. But you actually need to do these things. We talked about this."

"A blind date in a foreign country when you don't even know the emergency service number might sound like a jaunt to you, but to me, it's … scary."

"Blind dates are fun. Foreign countries are fun. And it's 9-1-1. You can do this. And if it goes wrong, you'll have a great anecdote for dinner parties. So when are you guys meeting?"

"I haven't texted him back yet. He wants to meet tomorrow night for drinks."

"Good. Do it. I'm going back to bed. Call me after. I'll want details."

"Wait!" I shouted, but she'd already hung up.

I sighed, stroking Saucy in my lap as I looked at the shopping bag with my dress inside. Then I navigated to Eric's message and typed in: *Sounds good.*

Once I'd written that I realised I had no idea, one, what Eric even looked like and, two, where in Miami The Cuban was. There must have been a hundred places called The Cuban, here? What if he looked like Donald Trump? What if The Cuban was in some back alley where people regularly got shot? This was America, after all. The Wild West.

Now, I had no choice. I'd soon be finding out.

NINE

To put to rest my concerns about The Cuban, I took a taxi from the Four Seasons and peppered the driver with questions about it, from the moment I slid into the back seat.

Unfortunately, my driver didn't speak much English. "*Donde ... esta—*" I fumbled, filtering through my limited knowledge of Spanish, before giving up entirely when my mind kept hitching on *la biblioteca?* It was too exhausting, and I was too nervous to think. If the place looked like a hovel when I arrived, I wouldn't leave the car; I'd ask the driver to take me directly home and call it quits on the whole thing.

Part of me *hoped* it was a hovel in the bad part of town, as I sat there, smoothing out the skirt of my dress. Saucy had been sad to see me go again and I felt guilty. I'd brought him for company, but I hadn't been home as much as I thought I'd be. It wouldn't have been so terrible to spend this Friday night in bed, eating directly from a carton of Chicken Balti and watching chick flicks. Maybe *The Hunger Games,* considering the mood I was in.

The Cuban wasn't in a terrible part of town. It was in the same area where Tori and I had stopped for drinks, a sleek, modern place, surrounded by valets, and elegantly dressed patrons. The women looked effortlessly chic in their frocks, dark sunglasses and high heels. I took a deep breath and looked down at my outfit, hoping I wouldn't be out of place.

There was a queue of cars, waiting to drop off at the front door. We joined the back of the queue and the driver pointed at the door and walked his fingers toward the curb, lifting his eyebrows suggestively. I squinted. "You? Go now?"

"Oh." I shook my head. Despite the way my thighs were sticking to the vinyl seat, I was very happy to stay in the car until the very last moment.

He smiled and inched along.

I sat there, fanning my face, trying to gather my courage. I was going to have to face Mr Blind Date sooner or later. No use putting it off. Better to rip it off, like a plaster.

My bravery suddenly deluged forth and I reached for the door handle. "Actually. Here's good."

The car lurched to a stop, taking me with it, my head almost hitting the credit card reader on the back of his seat. I shoved my credit card into it then pushed out onto the curb. "You can do this," I whispered.

"You can do this!" The driver parroted back, grinning with amusement. "*Buena suerte!*"

"I hope so," I said uneasily, as I steadied myself on the curb and closed the door. I stalked towards the double doors of the restaurant as a statuesque woman in a long scarf swept by me, consuming me in a cloud of perfumed air. She looked like one of the models who always visited the offices of *Slip*. They reminded me of cats, plumped with lip-fillers, exotic but also a tad frightening. I trailed behind her, wondering who I'd have to sell my soul to in order to look that chic.

I'd felt pretty confident, earlier that night, when I'd looked in the mirror. But right then, seeing groups of men and women, I felt awkward and paranoid. What if I choked on my food in front of him and had to spit it out, or worse, what if a waiter had to perform the Heimlich manoeuvre? That would be a shame too great to bear.

Oh, God. I can't do this.

I turned to head back into the car, but it'd already gone ahead. A stretch limo with tinted windows idled in its place.

Squaring my shoulders, I meandered past a couple of ostentatious golden vases at the front of the building, towards the sliding doors. pushing a lock of hair from my face as I approached the host's podium. I looked straight ahead, because letting my eyeballs volley around the place – like they wanted to – was a sure sign of how I was feeling. I wanted to create the illusion of a confident exterior. Just like Jessica had instructed me.

When the Adonis-beautiful host looked up from the podium, I said, "Benowitz," trying to keep my voice even. "I'm meeting an Eric? He's probably not here yet, since I'm—"

I stopped when he plucked a menu from the stand and said, "Right this way."

My eyes widened. "He's already here?"

The host gave me an inquisitive look.

Well, that was a surprise. I tried to take a step to follow the host, but my feet seemed to be cemented to the ground. "Uh. Is he hot?" I squeaked.

Adonis's face softened. "Not bad," he said with a sympathetic smile. "Blind date, huh?"

I nodded, my eyes trailing to a luxurious curtained passageway, beyond which might have been my future husband, a serial killer or something in between. I took a step, then stopped. My voice was quiet. "Should it not be going well, is it possible we might have a signal?"

The man hesitated. "A signal?"

"Yes. Suppose he's a Ted Bundy type?" I tittered, though I wasn't sure I should. Perhaps the Bundy comment was a bad joke. I didn't want to offend someone, again. "I mean, suppose he's a little off? Is there something I might do in order to have you escort me safely out of the restaurant?"

"Not to worry, I understand." He paused, thinking. "Sure. You can ask for clean cutlery if you need assistance. Okay?"

"Yes!" I said, relieved that the host was on my side, my guardian angel. Now, with the odds of me surviving this night significantly improved, I could just worry about whether my date expected sex.

Not that sex was on the table.

Or at least, it wasn't, until the host stopped at a table, and I looked down upon tumbling dark hair, a strong jaw with the slightest bit of stubble, and deep brown eyes, as heart-stopping as a coronary.

In short, Eric was definitely my type.

This has got to be the wrong table, I thought, even as the host pulled out the chair for me. I blinked a few times, then said, stupidly, "Is that for me?"

Adonis nodded. I plopped down on the seat like my backside was made of lead.

"Frankie?" the man said, thrusting a hand over the wine list, towards me.

I stared. *Okay, maybe sex is on the table tonight.* His eyebrows tented, and I realised I'd missed a question. I took his hand. "Uh, w—"

"I'm Eric."

"Oh. Of course, you are." I said, failing to keep my composure. "I'm Frankie."

I let his hand stay in mine a beat too long because before I realised what was happening, he was practically prying it free. "So ... you know Jessica?"

"Yes. She's a great friend of mine. And you know her, too?"

He nodded. "She made my flat downtown liveable. I work for B and B."

I couldn't imagine this dashing man, sitting in a dainty old Victorian home, folding linens, and serving popovers, but maybe I was mistaken. "You work for a bed-and-breakfast?"

He squinted. "For Bradford and Bradford. Only the biggest financial firm in America. I'm quite high up in the company. But I forgot. You're not from here. What are you doing in Miami?"

"Well, I have a position working in—"

Suddenly, he snapped his fingers. A waiter stopped, bending to his wishes. He picked up the wine list and scanned it. "We'll have the '58 Sauvignon."

"Right away, sir." The waiter scurried off, leaving me with traumatising flashbacks to Piers. He liked to order wine for us, too, like he was a professional sommelier. It was always embarrassing how pretentious he was when picking out wines.

He guffawed, a sound that didn't match his suave *façade* at all. I actually recoiled. "You don't mind me ordering? I'm kind of a wine snob."

I winced. *Here, I've barely tucked in my chair, and sex is already back off the table.* "No, that's fine. I'm not one."

It didn't matter what he ordered. Expectations of sex or finding a future husband dissolved, I decided to relax and try to have a good time. At least I'd get a free meal out of it.

Or …

"Geez, look at that," he said, lifting his wine glass to the light. "What a mess. You think a place this expensive would hire competent help."

I straightened to see what was wrong with the glass. "Is there something—"

More snapping. A waiter approached. "Get this taken care of."

"Yes, sir."

He smiled charmingly and leaned forward. "But don't worry about the price, princess. I've got this." He winked and his leg brushed against mine.

Then, suddenly, a cold hand landed on my knee and squeezed. Hard.

I jumped and pushed my chair away. "Well, Eric. It's been a pleasure, but I think I'm going to go."

He stared at me as if I'd willingly forfeited a million-dollar prize. "We haven't even eaten yet."

"Yes, I know. I ... actually forgot. I'm ... fasting."

I spun around and high-tailed it for the door, catching the eye of the host as I reached it. "No cutlery, then?" he asked.

I shook my head and waved. *Not unless I want to stab myself.*

Stepping from the air-conditioning to sizzling Miami heat, I sweltered, realising I should've called a cab from inside. I didn't want to go back in, though. Not with the blind date from hell there, waiting for me. I fished my phone out of my pocket and paced in front of the giant vases out front, watching the line to see if there was an empty cab I could hijack.

One pulled up, just as I connected to the taxi service. *Well, at least something's going my way,* I thought, as the door of the cab opened. A gorgeous woman in a flouncy blue dress and voluptuous curls stepped out. I couldn't wait to get out of this dress and slip into a bathtub with a glass of wine and something fattening from room service.

I leaned into the front window of the taxi. "Are you available?" I asked the driver desperately.

His eyes were hidden behind Ray-Bans, but I could only imagine he was rolling them at me. "Yeah. Get in."

"Thank you," I said with relief, holding open the door so I could slip in once the other party vacated.

I was so busy trying to escape as quickly as possible that I didn't notice the man holding the door until he said, "Frankie?"

I looked up. It was Michael.

For a moment, I thought it must've been his doppelganger, someone who just looked like him. Why else would Michael be all the way over here in Miami? But then, why would this doppelganger know my name? Perhaps I was hearing things. I expected the resemblance to diminish, the more I looked at him, but instead, the opposite occurred. Dark hair, inquisitive deep eyes, his lean body filling his custom suit like a second skin. As the seconds ticked by, he only became more and more Michael.

In my shock, I let the taxi door go. It swung wide open on a sea breeze, smacking me in the hip and sending me jumping a bit towards him, on the curb. He winced. "You all, right?"

The accent was there. That confirmed it. I wasn't seeing things. "Michael?"

He nodded. "Fancy meeting you here. I heard you'd flown to this side of the pond."

I smiled. "What on earth are you doing in Miami?"

"Your father didn't tell you? I'm here for a case." He seemed a bit embarrassed.

No, my father hadn't told me. Was this his way of trying to set the two of us up? Probably not, his associates went all over the world for cases, and he could scarcely keep track of them all. But it didn't matter. It was like a slice of home had been mailed to me, a care package. My smile widened as I shook my head.

"In any case, it's lovely to see you," he said, leaning in to give me a peck on the cheek. The second he did, and I smelled his citrusy, woodsy aftershave, I thought of the way we'd danced at New Year's, under the stars. I was right back there. A breeze passed over me at the memory of the dance, his body and the way he held me.

The cab driver leaned across the front seat. "You coming, lady?"

"One second, please!" I called.

"Meter's running," he muttered.

I rolled my eyes and turned back to Michael. He was such a sight for sore eyes, I wanted to hug him. "How long have you been in town?"

"About a week."

With that, my hopes fizzled. He'd been in town a week, had heard I was here, and never thought to look me up when he knew I'd be alone? Perhaps the New Year's Eve dance had just been a chivalrous dance with the boss's daughter rather than the romantic connection I thought it to be. Still, I'd have thought he'd call me while out here? *Maybe he's avoiding me.* It didn't seem like him.

I could've been having this date *with him,* instead of wasting my time with Eric the Ego. "Oh, well—"

"*Michael*," An impatient voice called from behind him.

We both turned to see the woman with the beautiful curls and the blue dress, glaring right at me. His date.

Oh.

I'd never seen Michael with a girl before, so I'd not ever thought of him that way. Dating. I suppose I always saw him as too bogged down, helping my father to have time for women. I certainly never thought he'd have a "type". But clearly, as it was for most men, "lethally gorgeous" was his type. It made me a little sad. Which was silly; it was my imagination which had *reserved* him for myself. Though I couldn't help but feel utter disappointment at the sight of his date. I thought if Michael was going to have a type, he'd go for someone more like … well … me.

She hooked her arm through Michael's and smiled sweetly up at him. She looked a bit like a cat, toying with her food before she ate it. "We're going to be late for our reservation."

"Right. Oh," he said, a bit awkwardly. He motioned to me. "Brooke, this is Frankie, a friend from back home."

She looked me up and down. If her eyes were knives, I'd have been shredded to pieces. "Nice to meet you." There were ice cubes in her words.

I smiled. "Likewise."

"Hey, so I'll call you. Maybe we can grab a coffee?" he asked. It was such a *Let's do lunch* kind of thing to say. Those phrases are usually so insincere. Reserved as a token, offered to someone you're trying to get away from. But coming from Michael, I knew he was sincere. Besides, he'd just made the invitation in front of the woman he was dating. If he said coffee, it was *just* coffee.

Another thing that made me a little sad. "Sure. Sounds great."

Gentleman that he was, he held open the taxi door for me as I got situated inside, closed the door, and gave me a wave. That smiling dimple of his, the last thing I saw as the taxi pulled away from the curb.

I settled back in my seat and texted Jessica: *Thanks for setting me up with that narcissist.*

She never responded. I didn't want her to. Room service, the bathtub and my fluffy hotel robe were calling to me. I was delighted to be spending the evening with Saucy after all.

TEN

The following day was probably the worst yet.

I was sitting in my cubicle, bored, thinking that it was only two hours and seventeen minutes until lunch, as I moved projects from here to there on my computer screen. Luckily, I'd had a day's reprieve from the stapler, so I was actually thinking it was a good day to be alive. Tori and I were planning on checking out the new taco place in the lobby, and I couldn't wait. So even though I was put out about the Michael situation, and that Jessica had never texted me back after the horrendous date she'd sent me on, I was in a pretty good mood.

And then, disaster struck.

The door to Gillian's office opened with a crash, banging against the wall behind it so hard that the building shook. I knew it was her because she was the only one on the floor *with* a door. The rest of us lowly plebians had cubicles. Then, her heels started clicking on the tile floor between the cubicles, sounding like a typist, banging out a strongly worded letter.

"Intern!" she shouted.

I stiffened since I was the only intern on the floor. At first, I was confused. Did she need me?

I started to pop my head up when her head appeared over my cubicle wall. Her face was bright red. "Hello? Intern?"

I eyed her until it hit me. She'd forgotten my name. I'd been here less than a week. Hadn't she been *Frankie—love it!* like it was the cutest name she'd ever heard?

Right now, she wasn't regarding me as *cute*. She was looking at me like I'd murdered her family. At that moment, I wished there was a crack in the floor I could slither into. "Yes—"

"Believe it or not, in this country, it's customary, when you're being called, to answer," she barked, her eyes going to the ceiling.

My mouth opened. How did one respond to that? *In this country, I also thought it's customary to address someone by their name.*

"Well, I—"

"Forget it." She stalked over to my computer and jiggled the mouse. Then she brought up a project I'd never seen before. "What is *this*?"

It looked like a project, obviously. But I don't think that was the answer she was looking for. My job was shuttling projects from person to person, making sure they got in the right hands—writing, editing, art department. Between rousing stapling sessions, I'd done it about a thousand times that week. But this one, the date was outlined in red. Obviously, because it had passed.

Oh.

That wasn't good.

I swallowed, trying to come up with a good excuse. *Well, I've only been here a week.* Or *must've been a computer glitch.* The truth also skittered through my mind: *I must've missed it. Sorry!* But looking at her face, rabid with anger, I was frozen. I couldn't say a word.

A bit of elevator music had been playing before, piped in from some invisible speakers, but now, it was silent. All sounds from the cubicles around me had ceased, too. I could imagine them all sticking their heads up, like prairie dogs, tuning into this excoriation. My heartbeat started to fill in, thudding so loud I thought it'd escape from my chest.

"It's late. Do you understand what that means? Someone's going to have to work overtime to fix your mistake. And trust me, they're not happy."

"Well, if there's anything I can do—"

"You've done enough." She spun on her heel and marched away, leaving me to gawk at the empty space where she'd been standing in horror and humiliation.

A second later, Tori came by. *I told you,* she mouthed.

I sighed. She had, and I'd witnessed a few things since then that had worried me. Mostly, people walked on eggshells around Gillian. You could hear it in their voices—a bit of a tremor as if they were trying to appease a snarling dog. They also avoided her, didn't include her in personal conversations, and didn't invite her out to lunches. When she walked into the common room, everyone else filed out. But I'd hoped that because I was the "quirky Brit" she seemed to love on the first day, I'd be immune to her wrath.

Apparently, I was wrong. Gillian was acting like I'd bombed half the readership simply by forgetting to check the box and send that article to the editorial department.

What was wrong with me? I'd been strong before. Once upon a time, before Piers, I would've apologised and not taken the public humiliation so personally. Instead, I'd laid down like a dog and whimpered.

"I need drinks," I muttered. "Many of them."

Tori nodded. "Absolutely! Let's do it! But—" Her face stormed over. "Sorry. I forgot. I have a dentist appointment after work. My crown's been giving me trouble."

"Oh." My shoulders slumped. I really needed a mojito, right then. Maybe two. Three?

She came over and gave me a light shoulder rub. "Don't worry. We've all been there."

"Have you?"

"Sure. She doesn't like any of us. She once yelled at me for putting a Post-it on her closed door instead of emailing her."

I wanted that to make me feel better. It should have, but it didn't. "It is my fault. I missed that article."

"So what? We all make mistakes. She seems to think she doesn't, though."

"She doesn't?"

"If she does, she blames it on one of us. Her favourite thing to say is 'I know I told you—' even when she didn't. So don't take it too personally."

I couldn't not. My cheeks burned from the humiliation. "Who is going to have to work overtime?"

She leaned in and looked at the article on the screen. "Dane."

Great. The one good-looking, eligible man in the place, and he officially hated me. *You're really making friends and influencing people, aren't you, Frankie?*

Well, good. He was a wanker, anyway. He'd actually grumbled at me when he found me in front of the water fountain, filling my bottle. Maybe it was best for him to be knocked down a peg.

So, I spent the rest of the day, wallowing, worrying, and wondering what I was doing on this side of the Atlantic. Because hello, if I wanted to stay demoralised and sad, all I had to do was stay in London. I'd arrived at *Miami Scene,* hoping to make a good impression, to advance the magazine's mission, but also, to start a new chapter of my life, one that was brighter, more successful … better.

And now, it felt like I'd come all this way to get more of the same misery I'd had in London.

I was so nervous about seeing co-workers who'd either look at me with pity, or yell at me for making them work overtime, that I didn't even get out of my cubicle to use the bathroom. I cancelled the taco date with Tori. Instead, I sat at my computer, hypervigilant, checking and re-checking my work to make sure nothing slipped by all the while desperately needing to use the loo. One more wrong move would probably get me sacked. The thought of going back to my dad with my tail between my legs was even worse than being hated by everyone in the office.

As I double-clicked on a job to send it to the art

department, my mobile phone buzzed. I glanced at it without interest, intending to ignore it, and then did a double take.

It was a text from Piers.

My heart stopped as I snapped my eyes back to it, sure I was seeing things. But there it was: *Hey, love. How are things?*

I stared at it. It'd been months since I'd heard from him. Months. And now here, out of the blue, he wanted to find out how I was?

I still thought of him. Of course, I still did. Our lives had been inextricably entwined for so long. But I'd gradually been getting better, a thing I'd been proud of. I'd only thought of him once, today, in fact, when I was getting my toast this morning and remembered how he loved it burnt and used to leave black crumbs all over the kitchen counter.

I pounced on it and texted back: *Why do you care?*

Immediately, I hated myself. I shouldn't have answered. I should've blocked his number. There was one reason why I hadn't: I still harboured hopes that he'd come back to me.

A fact that was confirmed when his response came back and made my heart flutter: *Because I miss you.*

My jaw hung open. It had been nearly three months since I talked to him. I'd been close some nights. I found myself writing out texts the size of Russian novels, berating him for what he'd done. Other times I wanted to pick up the phone and invite him over for one night in each other's arms despite how much he'd hurt me. But this is what I get, out of the blue? *I don't think so!*

Before I could respond, he added: *Perhaps we could go for coffee?*

He wanted to meet me. Did he not know I was in Miami? I supposed not; Piers wasn't one to concern himself with insignificant details, or any details, for that matter. I could never see him social media stalking an ex. Not that I'd been big on updating my social media recently.

But all of a sudden, his offer loomed there, a bright spot in my miserable life.

At that moment, I missed family, home and security so much that I wanted to cry. Piers missed me. He still thought about me, loved me. Maybe I'd been too rash, before. Maybe he'd learned his lesson. Of course, I'd heard the phrase, *once a cheater, always a cheater,* and *A leopard doesn't change his spots.* But sometimes people changed, didn't they? Humans were capable of all kinds of things.

And I didn't need this place. I looked around. Everything was so foreign. So not me. How could I ever expect to assimilate to a place like this? It was folly.

My father would be upset. But when I told him how miserable I was, he'd understand. I'd be back in London, with Piers, where I should be, and all would be right with the world once more.

I'll call him, I thought, gathering up my things. *I'll quit this job, and we'll go for coffee, and Piers and I will be engaged again by summer.*

Hoisting my purse on my shoulder, I marched out of my cubicle. I took two steps out of the doorway and stopped short when I got to the glass-windowed "fishbowl" conference room in the centre of the floor. Sitting at the head of the desk was Gillian and that prat Dane, laughing charmingly at something her guest had said. She was clearly flirting with him. I scowled at her, wondering if it'd be in bad taste to give her the finger as my big exit overture.

Then I squinted and looked closer at the guest. I could only see the back of his head and his shoulders, so I decided I had to have been mistaken this time. It couldn't have been …

But then he turned slightly, and I saw him in profile.

Yes, for the second time, he'd surprised me.

It was Michael.

ELEVEN

Seeing Michael there, in my office, threw me off my game.

Not that I was "on" my game to begin with, but whatever thoughts were in my head about Piers and our happily-ever-after went completely out the window.

It didn't compute, watching those two separate parts of my life, suddenly colliding. Strange enough that Michael was in Miami. But in my office? How? Why? Things were getting stranger by the day.

After that, I wandered back to my cubicle and sat down, straining to listen to anything they might be saying to each other. The most I heard was Gillian's high-pitched, grating laugh. I don't know why, but I kept imagining Gillian saying, *you'll never believe how absolutely inept our new intern is! She absolutely destroyed our latest issue!*

But then I realised that was silly. I doubt she talked about her staff to the executives.

And another silly thing? Those ideas in my head about getting back with Piers. He was the reason I'd had to fly halfway around the world from my home. *He* was the reason I couldn't show my face in London social circles anymore. *He* was the reason I was starting at the bottom at *Miami Scene,* with the boss from hell.

I grabbed my phone and, quickly, deleted the conversation with Piers.

Yes. One nil to me.

Then I scooched closer to the opening of my cubicle, straining to hear more of the conversation so I could put the pieces together. My father had worked his connections to get me this position, which meant that he likely had a business relationship with the publisher of *Miami Scene.* My father never travelled anymore, not since my mother's death. It made sense that he'd have sent his right-hand man, Michael, to Miami to handle the details.

If so, though, why hadn't he told me? Was it possible that Michael didn't know I was working here? Had my father never told him?

My mind was swimming with questions, and I needed answers. I was balancing precariously on the edge of my chair, trying to decipher the bits of the conversation I'd heard when I heard the fishbowl's door open. Gillian's horrid laughter rang even louder through the cavernous office space. She said something like, "Well, that's a funny thing! You Brits are so charming!" which made my stomach turn with memories of how *cute* she'd told me I was, that first day.

I couldn't hear his response, but I desperately hoped he wasn't flirting back. Sure, he wanted to stay on the client's good side, but he didn't have to go smarmy. Standing in front of the bank of elevators in the middle of the floor, she said, "Well, a pleasure, as always. Do stay in touch about the Anderson issue."

"I will," Michael responded. "Of course."

I popped out of my cubicle and, staying low, I managed to skirt around the rest of the cubicles and dash to the other side of the building. I peered out the door, waiting for him. I had to be sneaky so Gillian wouldn't see me and order me back to my cubicle. When the elevator door slid open and he walked inside, I quickly slipped in next to him.

He glanced over at me as the doors slid closed and did a double take. "Hull—hullo! Frankie?"

It was cute. I'd flustered him. "Crazy that in such a big city, we keep running into each other! Did you know I worked here?"

He tilted his head. "I'd—I'd heard something about it. Yes." He smiled. "Seems like you're in the right place, you being a writer and all. *Miami Scene* is a great product. I've been working with them for a while now. Is it treating you well?"

"Yes, it's great," I said, trying not to dwell on Gillian. The last thing I wanted was news of my screw-up to get back to my dad. "So how are you? Did you have fun the other night at dinner? Do you love Miami? I didn't even know you knew it well. You've been coming here for five years?"

He nodded and laughed, and I realised I'd practically assaulted him with questions. I couldn't help it; that's how I was when I got excited. But he didn't seem to mind. He

said, "Yes. Well, not well. It's a change of pace, definitely."
He smiled. "It's good to see you, Frankie."

"Same here. Seeing you made me miss London less."

"Yeah."

We smiled at each other for what must've been a beat
too long because awkwardness seeped in. We both looked
at the door and realised that because no one had pressed a
button, the elevator was hovering there, closed. He jabbed
the button for the lobby.

"Well, how long are you staying?" I blurted, before
thinking of that girl he'd had on his arm. Maybe his girlfriend. I was hoping we could spend some time together
before he left. *Coffee. Coffee is innocuous … but with the
potential for more.* Though I knew he wouldn't be the sort
to two-time, I was curious to explore where this could go
and get to the bottom of the mystery woman. "Maybe we
can go out for that coffee?"

"Sure … I'd like that. I'm here for the next month, at
least. I'll text you."

The doors opened. I stepped out with him because
there was someone else waiting, but I didn't want to stop
talking. I'd have to take the elevator back up to reality,
but for now, I wanted this happy London bubble to last
a bit longer. I thought of that New Year's dance and felt
that same warmth, the same feeling of *Everything's going
to be okay.*

"Where are you staying?" I asked, to keep the bubble
from bursting.

"Four Seasons. You?"

My jaw dropped. "Same! And you said you've been here a week? Funny we didn't run into each other there."

"Very."

"Maybe I'll see you there, since we're neighbours!"

"Yeah. Hey." He paused and his face turned serious. "I'd love to take you on one of those Everglade boat tours. See some alligators, or crocodiles, or whatever. Something very Miami-touristy, since that's what I am. Are you interested?"

It took me by surprise. "What about Brooke?" I blurted.

His brow arched. "Oh, her? Brooke's actually a long-time friend."

I had to wonder if that was code for, *we sleep together, but it's no strings.* Michael didn't seem like the type for that either, he was always so *innocent.* "An airboat?"

Tori had been settling me into Miami's party scene, but it would be good to see what else there was. "That sounds fun. Okay, I'd love to!"

He flashed that dimpled smile of his. "Great. This weekend?"

I nodded.

"I'll call you," he said, then spun around and took his shiny black briefcase out the revolving door with him.

I watched him until he disappeared from view on the city street and sighed. Now I had to go back and face Gillian and hope I didn't fuck things up any more than I already had.

TWELVE

I spun in front of the mirror in my hotel room, as Saucy watched from the bed.

"What do you think?" I asked. "Passable?"

Saucy tilted his head as if to say *You're leaving me again? I don't care what you wear, as long as you bring me home a nice treat.*

Of course, I didn't have anything suitable for traipsing about the Everglades and looking cute doing it, so I had to go shopping again. But because I didn't have much time, I'd picked up some khaki shorts and a plaid button-up tank top, and a big cowboy hat with a wide brim, without consulting with the store associates. I figured, this was the South, why not? And it looked cute, laid out on my bed.

Now I had it on, I wondered if it gave off farmer vibes. What did people wear in the Everglades, anyway?

There was a knock on the door. Saucy barked. My pulse sped up. I quickly sprayed a cloud of Coconut Pineapple body mist and walked into it, letting it fall upon my skin. *There. Perfect.*

I opened the door to find Michael standing there, in a way I'd never seen him before. I was used to seeing him so buttoned up. But now, he was wearing a t-shirt and … great, loose khaki cargo shorts. So at least part of my outfit was correct, but now we looked more like brother and sister. Although, he had on a baseball cap (how very American of him) and a backpack that looked rather like we'd be taking a week away, instead of a few hours. I wondered what could possibly be in it.

He smiled. "Hey. Love the hat. You look very—"

"American?" I asked, hopeful.

"Yeah. I guess. Like a cowgirl. It's adorable."

"So do you!" I said, giggling and wondering if anyone would even recognise us as tourists.

"Ready?"

I nodded, then held up a finger and rushed back into the hotel room to get my bag. Usually, I was the one with the kitchen-sink bag, but mine was dwarfed by his. I had to wonder if I was forgetting something. "Ready!"

I left a treat in Saucy's bowl and assured him that Karla would soon be there to walk him. Turns out Karla and I had a mutual love of dogs. Then Michael and I headed downstairs to the garage. Michael had a silver-blue convertible waiting that screamed Miami. It was just a rental, obviously, but I would've picked the same car. Gentleman that he was, he opened the door for me. I settled in against the cool, buttery leather. When he got behind the wheel, I said, "Do people actually see alligators on these rides? Or … crocodiles?"

"Both, actually. You know the Everglades is the only place on earth where you can find both alligators and crocodiles?" he said with a smile as he pulled out of the space.

"No—" I said, a bit worried as we set off, into the bright sun. "I wondered about that. All the news stories I read from this part of the world have alligators showing up in people's bathtubs, chasing them down the street, surprising them in the passenger's seat of their car on their morning commute—"

"I know. But I think that's an exaggeration. I've gone on several runs and have yet to have an alligator chase after me. Or a crocodile, for that matter." He winked. "Anyway, supposedly this trip is quite an adventure."

The second he started to pick up speed, I felt my hat taking flight, too. I clamped a hand over it. Maybe it wasn't such a great idea to wear a hat. But the sun was annoyingly bright, and in the convertible, there was nowhere to hide from it. My skin started to sizzle.

Oh, no. I forgot the sunscreen.

We drove along the coast, out of the city, and I got a great taste of the surrounding area. Surfers paddled in the calm mirror-blue waters, while children played on the white sands. Then we turned inland on Route 41, where the homes and structures gave way to flat marshes and sawgrass. Most of the roads were lined with small man-made canals. The humidity increased as we made our way inland, despite the whipping wind, I could feel it pressing against me. I grew tired of holding my hat on my head, so I pulled it off, letting the wind muss my hair. I'd forgotten to bring anything to tie it back with, so it kept flying in my mouth.

"This is beautiful!" I shouted over the breeze, and it was, though as I was speaking, I'm pretty sure I inhaled a bug. I wiped my tongue with my fingers and found its waterlogged carcass. Luckily, Michael didn't notice.

"Isn't it? The sun is killer though."

He didn't have to tell me that. I looked over at my bare shoulders. Maybe it was the light, but they already appeared pink. I wasn't like Piers, who browned like a toasted nut the second he stepped out on our vacations. Usually, after days of slathering on sunscreen, I'd amass a bit of colour which would promptly fade the hour I returned home.

It's fine. I'll wear my hat the moment we get there, and it'll protect me. Stop worrying.

Michael seemed to be more like Piers, in that respect. Only here a week, and he already had a formidable tan, like a California native. It looked absolutely delicious and healthy on him. I was jealous.

"So do you like the change of scenery?" he asked as he pulled off at a side street and the noise lessened. "Your father said he thought it was doing you good."

I smiled, imagining the two of them discussing me in the boardroom in London. As strange as it was, it was nice that they cared about me as much as the business. And my father had been doing well, too. He seemed happy every night when I called him. "I do. I think it does my father better to have me out of his hair. I hate worrying him."

"Just because you're not there doesn't mean he doesn't worry about you. In fact, you're all we talked about before I left. He was worried you wouldn't like it here."

I sighed. "He doesn't need to worry about me. I'm twenty-four."

"*You* worry too much about him. He told me how you were constantly watching over him, after your mum's passing. Let Alex handle things for a change."

I snorted. "Alex isn't exactly a mother hen. You know him. He's too busy living the bachelor nomad life. I haven't talked to him in weeks. I have no idea where on the face of this earth he is. Do you?"

His lips twisted. "I actually haven't talked to your brother in about that long, too."

"What?" I stared at him. Strange, considering they'd been best mates, growing up.

"We had a bit of a falling out, I'm afraid."

"You did? When?" I suppose it didn't matter. "Was it over a girl?"

He looked at me and let out a laugh. There I was again, asking a thousand questions in a single breath. "I suppose you could say that." He shook his head like he didn't want to talk about it. "But enough about that. Tell me. How do you like the job?"

I was dying to know the gossip. Perhaps Jessica could do some digging for me and find out the details. "Oh. It's … okay."

"Just, okay?"

I knew I should be gushing, in case word got back to my father, which it likely would. But I'd been stewing about the Gillian thing for a long time. "Gillian's a … strong personality. You two get along?"

"She's all right. A little brash. But I guess that's why she's the boss. Why? You don't like her?"

"It's not that I don't like her. It's that—" *I hate her with a fire worse than that of a thousand suns?*

"I get it. Have you done much writing for the magazine?"

"No. None." Oh. That was a perfect reason for disliking Gillian. I seized it. "Actually, the truth is that Gillian doesn't allow outsiders to write for the magazine. So even if I wrote something, I don't think she'd be interested."

"Really?" His face wrinkled. "That's not fair. You should write something."

I laughed. "I guess it's fine. It makes sense. It's not like I know much about the *Miami Scene,* anyway."

"Yeah. But you could write a great story. 'A Brit's first impressions of Miami.'" He shrugged. "Write about today."

That actually wasn't too terrible an idea. "You know, I might. Thanks."

"You're a brilliant writer. I've read some of your things for *Slip.*"

I blushed, surprised. *He had? Oh, probably the story that my father had hanging in his office.* "Thank you."

He navigated to the side of a road choked with long swamp grass. There were other cars, parked ahead and behind us, but I couldn't see any other buildings. Just flat, marshy land everywhere. It was only when I stepped out of the car that I noticed the small, squat shack in the distance, and the airboats, lined up along a rotten-looking dock. It looked so bare; not what I was expecting at all. There were so many tourists on that dock, dressed in their bright touristy garb, I feared it might collapse. A big sign on one side of the shack had a massive cartoon alligator and said: *SEE EVERGLADES WILDLIFE UP CLOSE!*

He joined me on my side of the car and said, "Seems we weren't the only ones with this idea."

I shrugged. "It's okay. I'm sure it'll be fun, anyway."

By the time we arrived at the dock, though, I was roasting. We lined up for our boat with a number of other tourists, mostly families and retirees. I felt a trickle of sweat snaking its way down my upper arm, but when I went to swipe it away, found an insect the size of my hand.

"Eee!" I cried, doing a freak-out dance to get it off me, my skin crawling. Apparently, they were attracted to coconut-pineapple body spray.

He looked over and laughed. Then he reached into his bag and pulled out insect repellent. "Luckily, the boys at the firm warned me about this," he said, holding it up. "Mosquitoes. Hold your breath."

I did. He sprayed. So much for coconut-pineapple. Now I smelled like a chemical plant. I suppose it was worth it. Mutant mosquito bites or smelling nice? It was a fair trade-off despite how much I wanted to remain alluring to Michael. "Thanks. You wouldn't have any sunblock in there?"

"Sorry." Of course not. He had a great tan after being here for a week! What use did he have of sunblock? "We could probably get some inside?"

By then, though, the guide was already loading the boat, instructing everyone where to sit. Fastening my hat on my head, I squeezed between a chubby-cheeked doll of a toddler who was wearing an American flag frock and eating a cherry ice-pop. "Don't be silly, I'll be fine. Hi." I smiled at the girl.

She studied me with a kind of disgusted interest, as one would regard a new species of insect. "You talk funny."

I smiled. So much for blending as an American. "I do, don't I?"

"Are you a farmer?"

"No … I am a writer."

She tilted her head, observing. By now, Michael was sitting next to me. "You look like a farmer."

Michael laughed. I laughed, too. I guess I did. She dripped icy red drops on my knees, the very colour of her tongue. I swiped them away, hoping my skin didn't end up holding that hue by the end of the day.

But then the driver took off, revving the airboat's massive propeller, and my hat whooshed off my head. Michael reached up, making a gallant attempt to catch it, to no avail. It blew aloft, over the patches of grass and marsh, into dark, alligator and crocodile-infested waters, somehow sinking like a stone, never to be seen again.

The good thing was, I didn't look like a farmer anymore.

THIRTEEN

"I'm sorry you lost your hat," Michael said to me for the fifth time as the boat pulled up to the dock.

"Oh, it's fine!" I said breezily because I didn't want to look like some spoiled princess.

But it wasn't. I didn't care about the hat, even though it'd cost a week's worth of internship salary. What I cared about was that my nose was now traffic light red, a beacon that could signal to ships, passing in the night. As the guide pointed out various wildlife and sights, I kept crossing my eyes to see. I hoped that maybe it was a trick of the light, and I'd be fine once we got indoors.

"Look at that turtle!" a little boy shouted from the back of the boat. Everyone, including Michael, craned their necks to see. I took that moment to touch it gently. Oh, it was definitely tender.

I'd had sunburn before, but clearly nothing compared to a Florida sunburn. I crossed my eyes again, noticing something disturbingly yellow. Was that a blister?

"You should've seen that turtle," Michael said as he sat down next to me. The guide tied the boat to the dock. "It was huge. Hey ... you're getting a little red."

"Am I?" I asked as if I had no idea. "I suppose I should've got that sunscreen."

He took my hand and helped me off the boat. "Let's get it, now."

"Oh, don't be silly, we're done."

"Yes, but I have a convertible. And I thought we could eat lunch al fresco?"

I nodded. "That sounds nice." I wanted to spend as much time in Michael's company as possible, even if that meant third-degree burns.

We went into the small gift shop, which was crowded with the same people we'd seen on the boat. There were plenty of gaudy t-shirts about alligators and bumper stickers that said *I SURVIVED THE EVERGLADES*. I thought of buying souvenirs for my father and Jessica but wasn't sure what to get. Eventually, I settled on a couple of little glass vials with alligator teeth in them. That, and a bottle of Hawaiian Tropic SPF50, and I was set.

But then I saw it. "Michael," I said to him. He was standing next to me, perusing the postcards. "Psst."

"What?" He looked up.

"That. You need to get that. I think you'd look good in it." I pointed to the alligator visor.

He tilted his head. "You think?"

I nodded.

He reached for the top of the rack and pulled it down, fastening it on his head. "You think your father would give me a promotion if I wore this to the office?" He smirked.

"Oh. Definitely."

"But really. You're the one who lost your hat." He studied the rack and pulled down a pink one, made for a child. "You should get one, too. Allow me to purchase this for you, Frankie. It's the least I can do."

Now, normally, I wouldn't be caught dead in something like that. But Michael had already broken the ice, looking so absolutely ridiculous in his hat, it emboldened me. I slipped it over my head and said, "A suitable replacement for the other hat, yes?"

"Definitely. It's a must this season. You wear it well."

I had to admit I felt like Audrey Hepburn, in *Breakfast at Tiffany's,* when she and George Peppard donned masks in the dollar store and skulked about. Of course, we didn't steal anything; Michael was too good for that. The woman at the check-out counter looked at us like we had three heads as we set down our wares, still wearing the ridiculous visors. "And the hats, too," Michael said, pulling out his wallet. "Don't forget."

I stifled a laugh.

"Thank you," I said to him when we went outside, grabbing the tube of SPF and slathering it on my face. "You have definitely saved me from having a crispy fried nose."

We stopped on the pier, and he took my hat off, then his, placing them in the bag. I pouted. "Oh, and you looked so fetching in that."

"Yes, as did you. But we don't want another catastrophe like what happened on the boat, do we?"

I nodded, conceding. We walked to his convertible. He

moved ahead of me to open the door for me. "Thank you, kind sir."

I went to slide into the seat but realised he was studying me closely. I looked up, into his eyes. Never had my face been so close to his. Even when we'd danced, we'd done so without a lot of eye contact. This, and without the help of champagne, had my arms growing flush with goosebumps. He peered down at me, and at first, I thought he might push a lock of hair from my face. Then I thought he might kiss me, but I'd thought the same thing during New Year's, only to be disappointed. I was still the boss's daughter, and he was nothing if not respectful of that.

So instead, he said, very gently, "Let me get this," and ran a finger down the side of my nose.

I blinked and noticed a glob of sunscreen on the pad of his finger. "Oh. Appreciated."

If there was a fire between us, the blob of sunscreen effectively put a damper on it. He said, "In you go." and I slid inside the car. He jogged around to the driver's side, and we were off. Ten minutes later we pulled into the parking lot of an outdoor grill. "I hear that you can't leave the Everglades without trying gator."

"Gator?"

"And key lime pie."

"I'll try the key lime pie, but I'll let you have the gator."

There was a sign at the door that said, *Please seat yourself.* Michael strode among the tables and chose one near the edge of the seating area, away from most of the people.

I would've chosen the same one. Interesting, considering every time I went out to dinner with Piers, he'd always choose the table I'd be least likely to pick, almost as if he knew it and wanted to go expressly against my wishes. Or maybe he chose the most visible spot in the room because he liked an audience, and loved telling stories in a loud, theatrical voice, involving everyone in the vicinity. But I liked to eat in relative peace and quiet. I enjoyed talking to strangers and getting to know new people, but a restaurant was for eating.

I sat down on one of the flimsy plastic chairs at the picnic table and opened my menu. "Oh, they have frogs' legs."

He said, "Tastes like chicken."

"You've had them?"

"I'm having gator. Let's not push ourselves, shall we?"

The waiter came and asked us for our drink orders. "I'll have a glass of white wine," I said, even though I was already feeling tired from the sun.

"Make that a bottle," Michael said. "And we'd like to try your fried Gator appetiser."

The waiter left, and I asked the question that had been burning in my mind since I saw him in my office, "So tell me. Did you ask me out as a favour to my father?"

He looked taken aback. "What?"

"I mean, it's okay if you did. My father has called or texted me at least once a day since I got here. He's worried about me fitting in, doing well for myself. Especially after what happened."

"What do you mean?"

"The broken engagement. You don't have to walk on eggshells about the subject. It's fine. I'm over it."

"You are?"

I nodded. "Of course."

"Actually, I asked you out because I remembered what you said to me on New Year's."

I frowned. "That was so long ago, *I* don't even remember."

"You seemed shocked that I'd gone on holiday by myself. I got the feeling it was the last thing you'd do. And so, I could only think that being sent here, on your own, couldn't have been your idea. And that you could use a friend."

"Oh. Is this charity, then?"

"Far from it."

"And yet you knew I was in town, but you waited a week … longer … to ask me."

There was a bit of a blush under his tan. "I was working up the courage."

I laughed. Him? Of all the people who needed courage. He wasn't ego, but he was quiet confidence. The man who didn't need all eyes on him to perform. "*Please.*"

"It's true. I would've asked you out in London, but—"

"My father. I get it."

He shook his head. "No. Your father … I actually think he wanted me to ask you out. That's why he always spoke of you to me. But then you and Piers—"

This was news to me. "Why didn't you … at New Year's?"

"I got the feeling the wounds with Piers were still fresh. You'd only just ended things with him." He shrugged. "I was waiting for the right time."

"Waiting? You could've asked me out before Piers. You've known Alex forever."

He chuckled. "That's precisely why I didn't ask you out, Frankie."

"Alex?" My eyes widened at the thought. "He wouldn't have cared."

"Trust me. He would've. I couldn't glance at you without him thinking I had a salacious look in my eyes. Your big brother is a bit of a tosser. But I guess he was always very protective of you?"

I stared at him. This was even more news to me. If Alex hadn't been so over-concerned about my love-life Michael and I might have started dating years ago. Then I never would've met Piers, and … and …

"You've been mates a long time. You should know by now not to listen to a thing he says."

"Ah, but he's not just a mate. We may have drifted apart in recent years, but he's probably my oldest and closest friend. And your father, my boss? Suppose things should go south with you? I'm putting the rest of my life in a precarious position. So it wasn't an easy decision to make, as much as I wanted to."

"And what makes you think things would 'go south' with me?" I said, with mock indignation.

He smiled. "If it did, it would be entirely my fault, I'm sure."

The waiter came with the wine and poured us each a glass. I slumped back in my chair, trying to absorb this information. He'd been interested in me. For years. And my sod of a brother had put the kibosh on things. I sucked down half the glass in one mouthful. "I can't believe this, Michael. I followed you and my brother around like a shadow from the time I could walk. You always acted like you were annoyed with me."

"Yes, well, you *were* rather annoying when you were a kid. And then—"

He seemed to have trouble finishing the sentence. What was this, the cool Michael, at a loss for words? I filled in. "Puberty?"

He laughed. "Well, yes. If you want to put it that way."

"And then?"

"Well, before I knew it, you were off to uni. And then you were with Piers. Then engaged. By that time, I was working all hours for your father." He let out a self-deprecating laugh. "I'm the king of terrible timing."

"Not anymore," I said holding up my glass and clinking it with his. "So what if it's late? Finding you here was an amazing coincidence. To the right place at the right time."

"Yeah." He looked down at his glass and took a sip. "But I want to know how we're going to get you writing again."

We. As if we were in this as a team. I felt a flush, a warmth in my chest that had nothing to do with the sunburn. Piers was always *I, I, I.* He certainly never had much to offer on career advice since he didn't want me working in the first place. Damn the fact that I actually enjoyed it, that it fulfilled me. Piers just wanted to know how I was going to fulfil *him*.

"I don't know," I said, finishing my glass of wine. "You think I should write about this? From a Brit's perspective?"

He nodded.

"And then what? Anonymously slide it under Gillian's door? I'm the only Brit in the building. She's going to know it's mine. And then she won't publish it, on principle."

"Do it. Have faith in your talent. If it's good enough, she might publish it. The worst she can say is no."

Suddenly, my fingers itched to write. I could imagine the bright scalding sun, the smell of the marsh, the squeals of the seagulls overhead, in perfect prose. It'd been a long time since I'd felt like I had anything to say. But could I do that? Take the risk of getting chewed out by Gillian again?

I shuddered at the thought.

Our fried gator came, right then, in a little red basket. Wanting to be the first to taste it, to show him how adventurous I could be, I reached in and took a strip, and gnawed off a bite. It was chewy in texture and slightly fishy, but other than that, it tasted remarkably like chicken.

"Not bad," I said, proud of myself. Trying new things wasn't so bad. And I was ready to take another chance, too. "All right. I'll write that article and see what happens."

He smiled. "Good. That's my girl."

His girl. I liked that, too.

FOURTEEN

After we finished lunch, Michael took me back to the Four Seasons. On the ride up in the elevator, he handed me my souvenirs as we chatted about how different things were on this side of the Atlantic. We also joked about how remarkable it was that not once did an alligator or crocodile chase us through the parking lot.

When the doors opened to my floor, he walked me to my penthouse room, and that's when it hit me.

Pure terror.

Funny, when I was thinking about the date with Eric, all I'd thought about was how we'd end the date. Would he be content with ending things with a handshake? A chaste kiss? Tongue? Or would he want the whole nine yards, dirty, all-night sex? But with Michael, I hadn't even thought about that at all. Michael was handsome, charming ... and yet I hadn't thought about sex with him. At least, not consciously. Maybe somewhere in the back of my mind, I'd thought about it, but it hadn't hit me that I'd have to deal with this situation with him.

Teeth chattering, I said, "I had a great time." I motioned to the door. "I'm actually really excited to write now."

"Then by all means, you should. But Frankie."

I'd been rifling through my purse for my key card. He took my hand, stopping me. I couldn't meet his eyes. "Hmm?"

He pulled me flush against him so I had no choice but to look up, into his eyes. "Let's do this again."

I nodded, my head bobbing like a puppet on a string.

Then he lowered his head and captured my lips with his own. Not a chaste kiss, but not lewd, either. Perfect. Like Michael always was. He tasted of peppermint which was funny since I didn't recall him eating one after our meal – and a little like wine. His lips were warm and soft and … like I said, perfection.

And for the smallest of moments, I wanted to throw my lofty ideas of writing to the wind and drag him to my bed, article-be-damned.

But he broke the kiss and stepped away from me, still holding my hands. "Happy writing, Francesca."

Francesca. It was even more delicious than when he'd called me Frankie for the first time, and that had nearly knocked me out. Now, my knees buckled and I leaned against the door for support.

He walked to the elevators and without looking back said, "Aloe for the sunburn."

All I could think was that I'd always hated it when people used my given name … until now.

• • •

Inside, Saucy yipped happily as I floated on a cloud to the bedroom. I stripped out of my clothes and put on my comfy lounge pants and a tank top, perfect writing-wear.

It was only then that I looked at my face and realised the extent of my sunburn. I had raccoon eyes from my sunglasses. Oh, I looked ridiculous. How had Michael looked at me with a straight face? *Kissed* me?

It didn't matter. I danced my way to my desk and pulled out my laptop. As I wrote, I kept glancing over at my pink gator visor or touching my lips. They still buzzed from where he'd kissed me. I could taste the peppermint, smell his citrusy, woodsy smell … his essence was all around me. The thought of him, saying, *You can do this. You can write this article* spurred me on, and the words flowed from my fingertips as if inspired by magic.

Eventually, I looked up from my computer and realised it was dark. I had a four-page article on everything Michael and I had done, from the gator tour to the key lime pie we'd shared. I read it over, and would have patted myself on the back if not for the sunburn on my shoulders. Humorous, entertaining, with my typical self-deprecating style, I knew it was some of my best work yet. If *Slip* had covered Miami attractions, they'd have published it in a heartbeat.

When I printed it out, I actually kissed it. I had tears in my eyes. It felt so good to get back into writing, like seeing an old friend I thought I'd never lay eyes on again.

After that, I was shivering and a little ill from the sunburn. I called the concierge and asked them to send me up a bottle of aloe, then took a shower and slathered the whole bottle on my tomato-red body. It hurt, and yes, there were blisters on my nose. But as bad as it was, I couldn't help grinning from ear to ear.

I needed to share my triumph with someone. So as I lay there, in relative agony, I dialled up Jessica on speaker.

"You know it's three in the morning, here," Jessica griped when she answered.

"Oops. I forgot. Again. But actually, I don't care much. You owe me. After Eric."

"How was I supposed to know you two wouldn't get along? He ticked the top two boxes on your list. He's good-looking and rich."

"That's *your* list," I reminded her. "I actually need someone with a bit of class, too. Manners. Who doesn't assault me under the table two seconds after meeting me."

"Oh, class, whatever. Give me a dirty, irreverent boy any day." She yawned loudly. "Why are you disrupting my sleep, this time?"

"I wanted to tell you. I went out with Michael."

"Michael. You mean … tall, dark and sexy, man-of-your-dreams Michael? From your dad's party? Isn't he your brother's friend and your father's employee?"

"That's right. He's here on business."

"And how was it?"

"Good. Really, really good." My heart fluttered at the thought. "I got sunburned."

"Aloe. But what about the man?"

More flutters. "He's nothing like Piers."

"That's a *big* check in the plus column. Did you have sex?"

Leave it to Jessica to cut right to it. "What? No! It's like a first date."

"But you've known each other forever. So, you could have."

"No. Michael's not like that," I said. "He's not like Piers. He kissed me, though."

"And how was that?" She sounded a bit bored. *She* would've shagged him.

"It was nice. Really nice." I didn't know how to explain it in words. "He's really—"

"Nice? Your vocabulary is terrible for a writer."

I sighed. I mean, obviously he was all those things I looked for. I could see that. Handsome, tall, rich, sexy ... with class! But it wasn't only that. No. There was so much more to it. Otherwise, I never would've fallen like I clearly had, after one silly date. It was something else. Something that had been smouldering beneath my consciousness for years was re-ignited.

It suddenly hit me, as I was stumbling over a way to explain it to her.

I trusted him.

Deeply. Unlike anyone else, except maybe my mum and dad. And that was something that I desperately wanted to be able to do with a man.

"You know, he got me writing again. After all this time. I wrote an article. I'm going to submit it tomorrow to *Miami Scene*."

"That's great, Frankie. I'm glad you're getting back into things. You should. You're a good writer. Despite your overuse of the word 'nice'." Another yawn. "Can I go back to bed?"

"Oh. Yes. Sure. Sweet dreams."

I ended the call and laid there on my bed, staring up at the ceiling, Saucy cuddled in the crook of my arm. I couldn't move—oh, the pain—but I could smile.

I think I was still smiling when I drifted off to sleep.

FIFTEEN

The following Monday, as I was on tenterhooks at my desk, praying to the Microsoft gods that I didn't make another critical error, I felt a presence hovering at the entrance to my cubicle.

I spun, expecting Tori. We had a lunch date; she'd wanted to finally get me down to the taco place in the lobby and hear all about my date with Michael.

But it was Dane.

I'd spent my time as an intern doing a little dance around the floor's most coveted man. If he came into the kitchenette to get coffee while I was heating up my lunch, I'd just stare meaningfully at my Lean Cuisine as it spun on the turntable, as if it held all the wonders of the universe, until he went away. When we saw each other in the hall, we quickly averted our eyes. As part of the exalted golden Editorial department, I rarely saw him, except through the windows of the fishbowl conference room, when he, Gabe, and Gillian gathered every Monday morning for their editorial chin-wag.

He stood there, posturing like he was posing for the front cover of a magazine, hand on hip, nose pointed down in a smouldering, intense gaze.

"You," he said, his voice low.

I glanced at the time on my phone. Wasn't the meeting now? What was he doing, here, in lowly intern no-man's-land?

"Me," I replied, fully aware that he'd probably forgotten my name. "Or were you practising different letters of the alphabet?"

He stared at me, unamused. "Funny." He tilted his head as if seeing me for the first time. One corner of his mouth raised slightly, in disgust. "What happened to you?"

I followed those ice-blue eyes of his to slightly under my chin, where my bare shoulders were in the process of turning waxy, like lizard skin. Layers of it were peeling from my body—my cheeks, my forehead, my shoulders. Even worse, I had a scalp sunburn, and now, I had what looked like the worst case of dandruff known to man. There were large white flakes, sticking up from my parting. I'd brushed my hair into a ponytail, but quickly realised using the brush was picking up the flakes, making it even worse. Eventually, I'd stuck on a giant headband, which helped hide it a bit.

Before I could ask him what part of me disgusted him most, he said, "Come on. Gillian wants you."

Oh, no. "What for?"

He shrugged. "Come on. Get your butt up and you'll find out."

I looked around, helpless. "Do I need to … bring anything?"

He gave me a look, like, *Hell if I know.*

139

As I grabbed a notebook and pen, the standard accompaniment for any meeting, it suddenly occurred to me what this was about. The moment of truth. I'd been expecting it, though not this quickly.

You see, I'd arrived bright and early that very Monday morning, when the floor was dark and empty, with my masterpiece: *Everglades Idyll: A Tale of a Brit in Miami.* I'd stealthily slipped it under Gillian's door, with a Post-it that said, *Hi, Gillian, I dabble in writing from time to time and was a staff writer for Slip magazine in London. I thought I'd give you right of first refusal on the piece I wrote this weekend. If it's not for* Miami Scene, *no problem. Thanks, Frankie.*

The thing was, I knew my article was *exactly* the kind of thing *Miami Scene* published, the same tone, the same length, everything. I'd done my research over the past few weeks. If she didn't want to publish it because of some vendetta she had against me, or because she was some snob about letting employees "stay in their lane," fine. But Michael was right. I'd kick myself if I didn't at least try.

Now, though, as I walked behind Dane toward the fishbowl, I wondered if I'd made a huge mistake. Would she fire me for the attempt, for even daring to believe that I could be one of them? As I walked, I caught sight of Tori, peering out from her cubicle, looking as if she'd seen a ghost. *I'm sorry,* she mouthed, pre-emptively.

I tried to smile at her, but my face was frozen in terror. Had they *ever* allowed someone into the mysterious, mystical world of their editorial department meeting? I'd never seen anyone else in there, except Michael, last week. In fact, a lot of times, Tori said they kept the blinds closed, so they could've been having an orgy in there, for all anyone knew.

If Gillian didn't want the article, all she had to do was toss it in the garbage. That's what I'd expected. I'd tell Michael, *Oh well, I tried!* and go back to my miserable interning existence. But I was so sure that she was pulling me in there to call me out in front of the rest of the editorial department and excoriate me publicly. Possibly put me in chains and string me up in the lunch room so people could spit on me as they waited for their microwave meals to heat up. My palms were slick with sweat, and my headband suddenly felt far too tight.

When I got to the fishbowl, the blinds were drawn. I felt like I was entering a cave of enlightenment, where many people entered, but few returned. Or ... an orgy? I wasn't sure what was worse.

Inside, Gillian and Gabe were both tapping on their laptops, oblivious to our entrance. Thank goodness, they were still clothed. Dane looked at me and motioned to one of the empty seats, across from the three of them. I felt like I was in a job interview, or more accurately, in front of a firing squad.

After I'd been sitting and sweating for about five minutes, my entire body itching from the sunburn but too afraid to scratch myself because I didn't want to make any sudden movements and disturb them from whatever they were working on, Gillian looked up. She seemed surprised to see me.

"Ah. Frankie."

At that moment, she didn't sound angry. But I knew her emotions could turn on a dime, so I braced myself, fingernails digging into my thighs.

She opened a folder next to her. I recognised the font, the title on the paper at the top of the small pile inside it. It was my article. Her eyes settled on me, superior in every way.

"I read your article."

Oh, shit, here it comes … I should withdraw it now.
"Yes, about that. I'm sorry, I should—"

"It was entertaining." She looked over at Gabe and Dane. "We all thought so. Right, men?"

Gabe nodded at his computer screen. Dane, slouching in his chair like some too-cool teenager, looked up at the ceiling as if to say, *I could've done better,* and shrugged.

"Yes, we were impressed," she went on. "And we're not usually impressed."

I stared, absently scratching at the side of my head. As I did, it was like a veritable snowfall, the flakes puffing up everywhere. Gabe looked absolutely horrified. I quickly dropped my hand and managed a glance at Dane, who looked about as *unimpressed* as I'd ever seen anyone, playing with a loose thread on the sleeve of his t-shirt.

"So … you liked it?" *Okay, stop acting so stunned, Frankie. You wrote for a reputable publication in London. Own your talent.* "Well, I did work for *Sl—*"

"So we'll send you the contract for February." She went back to her computer.

"Feb ... you mean, it's going to be in the February issue?" I blurted, again, far too excited than any professional writer, with several credits to her name, should've been.

"Mmm-hmm." She tapped on her computer some more, then looked up. "That's all. You can go."

"Oh. Thank you."

I got up and started to scurry away. When I had my hand on the doorknob, she said, "Oh, Frankie?"

I stopped, waiting for her to tell me I'd done something wrong.

She scanned me from head to toe, tapping on her chin as if she was trying to figure out what was wrong with me. "You know what? You should probably sit in at this meeting on a regular basis. It might be good for you."

"You ... want me to ... sit in?"

She nodded and motioned back to the chair.

I did as I was told. It was like receiving an invitation to royal court, or to sit with the cool kids during lunch. For the past few weeks, all I'd heard about from Tori was speculation on what Gillian and her editorial team did to run *Miami Scene.* Now, I'd been asked to join them. Sitting down, I set the pen down and laced my fingers on the pad in front of me to keep them from shaking.

The rest of the meeting was in secret code. Well, not really, but it might as well have been because I had no idea what they were talking about. Gillian barked out an order, like, "The Parker?" and either Gabe or Dane said, "Check." Sometimes she'd bark out a number, and one of them would say, "Covered." I assumed it was articles or pages of the magazine. I sat there quietly, wondering exactly *how* this was good for me. There were probably a bunch of jobs I was supposed to be clicking on, at my computer, and was right now missing. I wondered if this would come back to haunt me.

After about half an hour, the meeting ended. I stood up quickly and started to head back to no-man's-land. As I did, Gillian stopped me. "So? What do you think?"

She smiled with pride, as if she'd just shown off her newly-birthed baby, so I couldn't respond negatively and truthfully, with what I was thinking: *I have no clue what that was all about.* "It was interesting."

"I think maybe you should come every week. We probably need someone with your writing talent on board," she said.

I blinked. "Really?"

She snorted. "You don't want to be an intern all your life, do you?"

"No, of course not," I said, practically jumping into her arms. "Yes. Thank you. I'll be there."

I was smiling ear to ear as I went back to my cubicle. I peered in Tori's, but she was gone. Then I realised it was after twelve-thirty. I'd missed most of our lunch hour, and sadly, tacos and gossip with Tori. But my career aspirations had taken one giant leap, and my body was prickling with goosebumps over the possibilities.

When I got to the opening of my cubicle, I almost jumped back.

Dane was sitting in my chair, making himself at home. His arms were crossed and he was looking around the place, one eyebrow raised significantly higher than the other. He seemed utterly bewildered by my *Teacup Pups* wall calendar and the vat of aloe I'd brought for my sunburn.

"Do you mind?" I said, shooing him out of my chair.

As he got up, I noticed the chair was coated in flakes of my skin. I grimaced. He looked at my teacup, then swiped the photograph of me with my parents on my graduation from uni and stared at it. "So—"

I rolled my eyes. "Frankie."

"Right." He set the photo down without comment. "So, since Gillian thinks that you should be added to our editorial department, I was thinking … and I think you and I need to go out."

There was so much to unpack in that sentence, I barely knew where to start. "She's not adding me to the editorial team."

He smirked at me. "What do you think that was?"

"I'm still an intern."

"You can call yourself whatever you want. But no intern has ever been invited to our meetings," he said with a shrug. "So, you're in. The big leagues. Thus, let's go out."

"Out? Why?" His reasoning for our "going out" infuriated me.

He was looking at my dark computer screen, on Sleep

Mode, when he swiped a stray lock from his forehead, captivated by his reflection. "Because you need to know how the department works. And I can teach you."

Funny, before Michael, I might've jumped on the Dane Bus, without hesitation. After all, those blue eyes were like ... hypnotising. Not to mention the rest of him was so intimidating that I had a hard time looking at him without blushing. But his magic, his allure, was gone now. All I saw was a very Piers-like being, who only cared about himself.

"I'm sorry. Thanks for the offer, but I'm sort of seeing someone."

Even if it wasn't technically true, as one date barely constituted "seeing someone," I knew it was the right choice.

"That's all right. Like I said, it's purely professional," he said, not dissuaded at all by the rejection.

Oh, was it? Well, I suppose then, it might be—

"And if we do fuck, I won't tell anyone." He was still fussing with his hair in my computer screen.

My mouth opened. He wasn't serious. *Was there a punchline to that?*

I rolled my chair toward him, over his foot. "As appetising as that sounds, no."

Now, he looked a bit surprised as he pulled his foot out from under the roller wheels. I got the feeling he didn't get much rejection once he wore through the typical female's "hard to get" façade. Piers was the same way. He shrugged and strutted off, calling over his shoulder, "Well, you let me know when you change your mind."

Not if. *When.*

How about never? I thought, and I turned back to my computer to resume my clicking. As I did, I noticed I had a text. It was from Michael.

Hey. Thinking of you. What if we do something this weekend?

I smiled. Two dates. If that wasn't "seeing someone", I didn't know what was.

SIXTEEN

"Ohmigod!" Tori said as she sipped down her margarita. "You're not serious!"

Since lunch tacos hadn't worked out, it only made sense that we go out for happy hour. We'd collected Saucy after work, and settled outside The Flamingo, sipping fruity drinks and listening to a Cuban jazz band.

"I'm dead serious. Dane propositioned me."

"And you said no?" When I nodded, she pounded the table with both hands. "Oh! I would've *killed* to see his face! No one says no to him. Most women would give their left boob for a night with him."

"I got the feeling he does *plenty* of asking, and usually doesn't get turned down," I muttered. "But as attractive as the offer was, I have my sights set elsewhere."

She leaned forward. "Right. So Michael. Tell me all about it."

I smiled, thinking of the kiss. I'd replayed it in my head, again and again, and still, I couldn't think of anything other than "nice." Because words didn't, couldn't describe it, so why try? "We had a great time. And he's nothing like Dane, or … most guys. He cares. He's a family friend and he knows me. So I know he doesn't want me for a quick

148

fling or my inheritance. He's encouraging. I mean, he was the reason I actually wrote last weekend, for the first time in forever."

"Sounds good," she said with a sigh. "Like a one-in-a-million. I hope you're seeing him again."

"This weekend. I think he's taking me to the beach." I grinned at the thought. "I thought, since Gillian liked my last article on the Everglades, I could write one about the beaches, from a British perspective."

The sun had already set behind the buildings. She sat back in her chair and pulled off her sunglasses, then shook her head in amazement. "I can't believe Gillian actually loved what you wrote. I mean, I *can*. I'm sure you're very talented. But like I said, she never likes *anything*."

I shrugged and put my lips around the straw of my mojito, then pulled back suddenly. "But she must like something! How else would Gabe and Dane be on the team?"

"She likes Dane's *butt*. And his dimples. He's her Man Candy. I wouldn't be surprised if they—you know, on the side, when they have no one else better to do. And I think Gabe is her sister's kid, so nepotism." She shrugged. "So you? You are a unicorn. You must have the talent!"

I straightened my spine, full of pride. "I hope so. I can't believe my article is going to be in the February issue."

Tori beamed. "I'm so proud of you. Breaking the *Miami Scene* glass ceiling, only three weeks in. I bet you won't be in intern hell for much longer, with the way you're climbing the ladder!"

That thought—with the help of three mojitos— made

me feel giddy for the rest of the night. When Tori dropped me off at the Four Seasons, I took the lift up, happier than I'd been in *years*. I couldn't believe I'd waited this long to move on from Piers. That I'd been so stuck, thinking my life was over when our engagement ended. Now, I had so much. I had Michael. I had a budding career in writing. Everything was going my way.

When I reached my door, I saw a piece of paper stuck below the peep hole. It was Michael's handwritten signature, and my heart jumped. *Sorry. Just stopped by. Didn't want to wait till Friday. I'm 3608, in case you wanted to know.*

I practically giggled. How cute was he? He was thinking of me. Piers *never* thought of—

Oh, *fuck* Piers. Who cared about him?

When I went inside, I scooped Saucy up and danced him around the hotel room. I didn't want to wait, either. Plus, it was only eight. I could take a shower, put on my sexiest outfit, and stop by, too. The mojitos fuelled me with enough courage that I was more excited than nervous.

But as I was heading toward the shower, my phone began to ring in my hand. For the first time in a long time, when I looked down and saw the name *Piers,* I smiled. Of course. His ears must've been burning.

It must've been the mojitos because I picked up. "Yes?"

"Hi, Frankie. How are you?"

"I'm fine," I said shortly.

"What are you doing?"

"Truthfully? Wondering why you're calling me."

There was a pause. "I told you before, Love. I miss you. I asked about coffee. You never texted me back."

That was right. He missed me. I'd received that text days ago, and at the time, it'd felt like a lifeline. I'd wanted to jump on it. I wanted to take the next flight back to London and pick up where Piers and I had left off.

Was I insane?

Now, I could see everything so clearly. Isn't that why my father and everyone had wanted that distance for me? Because taking a step back allows you to see the whole picture.

And I saw it. Perfectly.

"Well, of course I didn't, Piers. You may not have heard, but I'm in Miami. So coffee is out of the question."

He chuckled. "Believe it or not, Frankie, I knew you were in Miami. I've known all along. It doesn't frighten me that you're there. There are ways of bridging the distance."

I frowned. "What if I don't want to?"

"You don't miss me? Not even a bit?"

I sighed. Yes, I missed him. Parts of him. Like waking up next to a warm body when it was freezing outside. The security of knowing someone would always be there, no matter what life threw at me. The ring on my finger that told everyone else that I was important enough to have been claimed by another person. But the last thing he needed was the ego boost. "No."

More chuckling, in that teasing way that made me feel like he could read my mind. "You're lying."

I sighed. "I'm not going all the way back to London to have coffee with you, Piers."

"Then I'll come there."

He said it so quickly, so surely, for a moment I was almost fooled into believing he'd turned over a new leaf. Since when did he cross a *street* for me, much less an ocean?

He must've sensed my hesitation, because he added, "I need to tell you how sorry I am. To see what I can do to win you back. We had many years together, Frankie. Good years. You owe me that, at least. Give me a chance to show you I've changed."

I swallowed. Two weeks ago, I'd probably have jumped into the Atlantic and swam there, to see him. But right now, I couldn't think. "Piers, no. Don't do this."

"I thought perhaps our relationship was important to you?" he said, his voice suddenly hollow. "We were engaged, after all. I never saw this as some kind of teenage relationship that can end with a snap of the fingers."

"I know, but—"

"I thought you cared about me? We're at least friends, aren't we? Or are you that cold? That you wouldn't even do me the courtesy of a second chance says a lot about you. It reeks of selfishness, Frankie."

Once again, I felt myself falling into the familiar position I always assumed with Piers. Always on the defensive, always on the back foot. Like I was the one in the wrong and the reason we'd broken up was over my mistake and not his. And yet somehow, even though I knew we were heading down that path, I still couldn't summon the courage to slam the door. *He missed me.* How many days and nights had I dreamed of hearing those words from his lips? Doesn't every spurned lover want to hear *Please give me another chance?* Even if it was in Piers' typical, self-important way, that was essentially what he was saying. "Piers. I'm tired. Can't we talk about—"

"Tired! It's nearly two in the morning here, love. You don't tell me about *tired*! I can't sleep without you here. Life isn't the same, Frankie."

Two in the morning. Suddenly, it hit me. The not-quite-right slur of his words. The grand pauses between his thoughts. The excessive emotion.

He was drunk.

No, he wasn't thinking about me, not in the obsessive way I'd thought about him, night and day, until I'd gone nearly mad. In the morning, he'd wake up, and he wouldn't miss me. In the morning, he'd roll out of bed, get himself some strong coffee, and go on with his life. He probably wouldn't even remember making this call.

"Good night, Piers," I said, jabbing the End Call button and tossing my phone on my bed.

At least now, I had better things to do.

SEVENTEEN

I knocked on Michael's door about twenty minutes later, Saucy under my arm. I'd been shaken by Piers' call, but now, I was more incensed, and it must've shown on my face because his appeasing smile fell the second he opened the door. "What's wrong?"

"Oh, nothing," I said, breezing into his room, though my voice was tinged with sarcasm. "How are you?"

"Fine—" he started, eyeing me cautiously as if I were a live grenade.

I looked around the room, desperate to be normal, to forget Piers. I put Saucy down and immediately he jumped onto the sofa and made himself a nest to snuggle down.

"Who's this?" Michael motioned to the little furry on his chair.

"Oh, that's my number one man, Saucy."

"Cute." He said as he bent down to stroke his ear. "Guess I'll have to settle on being number four."

"Four?"

"After your father and Alex, of course."

"Oh." I looked around, somewhat distracted, and my eyes landed on a tiny double bed. Sadly, as small as it was, it still managed to take up most of the room. There wasn't much else. The place was the size of my shower, upstairs. The walls closed in on me. I'd never been claustrophobic before, but right then, I felt it.

I fanned my face. "Goodness, why do you keep this place closed up?" I asked, heading toward a door next to the TV. I opened it up and found myself staring at another door. My head went faster. The room started to spin. I felt like I was trapped in some funhouse. "What is this? Where is the rest of your room?"

He smiled slightly, took the door, and shut it. "The connecting door. To another room?" My face must've revealed I had no idea what he was talking about because he said, "Believe it or not, Frankie. Not every room at the Four Seasons is a penthouse suite."

"Well, I—" I paused. I'd never actually considered that. "But my father would've paid for a—"

"Of course. But I don't see the need. It'd be a waste of your father's money since I'm rarely here."

"Yes, but—" I froze. *Wasting my father's money?* No one had ever said that to me. With Piers, it was always the best of everything. He'd never turned down anything offered by my father.

He caught my confusion and let out an abrupt laugh. "You've never—"

No, I'd spent my life in suites. I didn't know places like this existed. This seemed cruel and unusual. How did people breathe in prison cells like this? He cut off the question before I became too humiliated, took my hand, and led me to the thick, room-darkening curtains. Pulling them back, he opened the sliding doors to a postage-stamp-sized balcony.

I shook my head. "Oh, no. That's worse."

He lifted an eyebrow in question.

"I'm … not big on balconies. Or heights in general."

"Is that true? How did I never know that?"

"I don't know. I don't go advertising the fact on any billboards, so that's probably why."

He took a moment to consider this. "But I'm sure your penthouse has great views."

"Yes. And I do see them. That's what windows are for."

That seemed to perplex him. He hovered there, still holding my hands. "Would you rather leave?"

"No," I said immediately. I'd moved out to Miami to escape the things that had been holding me back. But I also needed to break free of my fears. I looked back at the tiny room, then at the balcony, trying to decide whether I wanted to start with my claustrophobia or my fear of heights, first. Funny, I hadn't even known I was claustrophobic. None of this had ever bothered me until now.

Then I took a step toward the doors. Beyond the railing, the lights of the other buildings seemed to swirl in the darkness, like a black hole. I hesitated, my hands that were clinging to him for dear life were slick with perspiration.

He slowly guided me out there and sat me in a chair, where the cool breeze greeted my lungs. I sucked air in greedily, then exhaled, slowly. After a few rounds, I felt better.

I said, "Why is your room so small?"

He chuckled. "I think it's that your room is so big."

"But you're here for a month! How can you—"

"Simple. I only use the room for sleeping. And I spend a lot of time out here. It's nice."

"But this is small, too ... and ... terrifying. It could break off and we'd plummet—"

"I can't believe you're on the top floor of this building and you don't even take advantage of your balconies. That's a shame."

"It's not a shame, because I will be secure in the knowledge that I won't fall to my death."

"But how often does something like that happen? Sometimes, it makes sense to take a risk. Because of the reward." He looked out over the railing and breathed in deeply. "I mean, damn. Look at this."

"I can see it through the windows."

"But not like this."

I shuffled to the edge of the chair and looked out over the railing. The ocean was spread out in front of us, separated from the night sky by a thin, hazy line. A cruise ship was heading out, lit up like a Christmas tree. I might have had bigger windows from which to watch the waves, but he was right. It was better out here. I felt more a part of it, like things were happening *with* me, as an active participant.

"Piers called me," I admitted, trying not to look down at the dizzying depths, below.

He sat down on the other chair, next to me. "Ah. And what did he want?"

"I'd say that he wanted me back, but that isn't it. He wanted to fuck with my head. That's all."

"So—"

"I hung up on him." I looked at Michael. "It's over."

I watched him carefully, expecting more of a reaction. I didn't get one. He simply nodded very slowly, calculating. For the first time, I noticed he was wearing crisp white tracksuit bottoms, and a t-shirt. I'd never seen him look so deconstructed. But his mind was classic Michael—it was almost as if I could see the gears turning in his head, weighing what this information could mean.

"Do you have any reaction to what I said?" I prompted.

He glanced up at me. In the dim light, his eyes reflected the pink light from a nearby hotel sign. "What do you mean?"

I shrugged. But the truth was, I'd hoped that my admission would peel away all obstacles that he'd seen before us. That he'd be spurred into action and would jump up and take the initiative. Sure, the kiss had been nice, but I wanted more. I'd been thinking, ever since Michael pressed his lips against mine, about more. The shoebox room inside wasn't good for much, but it did have a bed, at least.

But that was something Piers would've done. And Michael wasn't Piers, thank God.

So I summoned up the courage and blurted, "Do you want to kiss me again?"

Again, silence. But thankfully, his calculations didn't stretch on forever. A second later, he nodded.

He stood up, took my hands, and lifted me to standing. My breath hitched as he swept a hand through my wind-blown hair, pushing it from my face. Then he tucked a hand under my chin, lifting it to him, and kissed me lightly.

"Better?"

"More."

He chuckled. "All right. Soon," he said, turning me toward the view and wrapping his arms solidly around me from behind so I could feel his whole body pressing against me. "I've got you. So what do you think?"

The fear drained away, replaced with something new. Need. "It's nice."

He leaned in, his breath warm, and this time his mouth was on my neck. And he was kissing me there. I tilted my neck to the side to give him more room to roam, and he used it. He nibbled his way down my neck, coming in contact with the tie for my halter.

"Frankie," he whispered as I melted up against him, no longer afraid, but completely secure. "Are you sure you want this?"

I settled against him, savouring the question. It was a question foreign to me, one Piers never would've asked. Michael didn't just take. He gave. The thought made me shiver because I knew I was in for an experience unlike any I'd ever had in my life.

I nodded with certainty. "Absolutely."

In the next second, he whirled me around. His eyes locked on mine and a thrill of exhilaration surged through me. My heart pounded and my fingers trembled as I slowly traced the outline of his perfect, full lips. Desire pooled like hot lava in his eyes, and the touch of his skin was pure electricity.

Without hesitation, our mouths crashed together. The second my lips connected with his, that scared feeling of being a stranger in a foreign city went away. Now, I knew I was in the right place.

I kissed him softly at first, savouring the feel of him, the cool smoothness of his lips and rough stubble on my skin. He was even more beautiful up close. I brought my hands to his face, discovering the planes of his cheekbones, the line of his jaw, drinking him in with every one of my senses. Our tongues danced together, slowly, seductively, his thick, muscular arms tightening around me, crushing me to his rock-hard chest.

I arched up against him, claiming his mouth with my own power, and Michael groaned. The sound sent me spiralling, shivering, and I felt heat pulsing between my thighs. His hands gripped me tighter, and I felt his control with every ragged breath.

Dizzy and reeling, lost in a rush of fire, I didn't come up for air until I absolutely had to, until I couldn't tell whether the fire in my chest was from lack of breath or from him. When I did, he pushed me up against the wall of the balcony, once again knocking all the breath out of me. His hands moulded to me.

"I didn't ask you here so I could fuck you," he murmured into my skin as his tongue trailed down my jaw line.

I almost laughed. Piers would have done so and freely

admitted it. It was clear Michael had many, many admirers, like that "friend" of his he'd gone to dinner with, and he probably got a lot of sex. More than I'd had, for sure. But did it matter what his reasoning was? I wanted this. Wanted more of him. As much as I could get.

"I know, but I want you anyway," I murmured back.

He drew away a few inches and his gaze was filled with warmth. "Really? Have you—" His eyes held mine. He didn't need to say more, because I knew what he was asking. *Have I had any lovers since Piers?*

I shook my head. "But I want this. I want you."

That was all the permission he needed. He pulled me closer and continued exploring my body. I slid my hands under his shirt and ... oh my goodness. My jaw dropped open as I felt the ridges and valleys. There wasn't an ounce of flab, anywhere. Where had this come from, and why did he feel the need to always hide it with a suit?

He pulled his shirt over his head, and as much as I wanted to feel his skin against mine, my eyes wanted to feast on the glory that was his naked torso. He was incredibly cut, tanned, with dark hair smattered over his pecs. I ran my fingers through the warm field of hair, then pulled him to me, bringing our bare skin deliciously together. The heat was almost too much, sending the rest of my body screaming for more.

He kissed me desperately, hungrily, leaving my knees weak but every pore in my body operating on full overload as he traced my skin with his fingers. Dipping his head down, he kissed my neck again.

I lost it. I arched my back and my head fell back as if on an oiled hinge, and I gasped.

My body was going to explode with need. But he wasn't doing this to me. We were doing this, together. And I was happy—so deliriously happy—to let it happen because I knew it was right.

"Are you okay to go inside?" His voice was low and husky.

Inside? Why wouldn't I be okay to go inside? I couldn't remember anything about what we'd talked about. I'd been afraid about something … about to have a panic attack. But right then, as my eyes fell on his lips, those amazing lips that had kissed me senseless, it fell away. God. The lips were beautiful, but just the start of the beautiful things about him. I could barely look at his chest head-on, because it was like something Michelangelo might've sculpted. Over twenty years of knowing him, and how did I never notice this glory?

"Inside?" he asked again, leaning in to nuzzle my cheek with his lips. I realised I hadn't answered him. I was a puddle of goo in his arms.

Yes, yes, yes. Inside, on your bed, let's do this. But words didn't come out. Instead my face fell forward, seeking out his lips. I traced his bottom lip with my tongue.

He kissed back. His tongue entered my mouth, not invasively, not as though he was staking a claim. No, we had equal parts in this kiss, as if he wanted me to own it, too. At first, I let him kiss me, unsure of what to do, but then, my instincts kicked in. I laced one arm around his neck and put my other hand in his hair, pulling his face closer to mine. Hugging him tighter to me.

Then I wrapped my legs around his waist.

He adjusted my position slightly so my warmth was perfectly aligned with his hardness then wrapped his arms around me, pinning me in place. He broke the kiss and took a ragged breath, just long enough to say, "So that's a yes?"

I let out a moan that was supposed to be a yes.

He carried me inside, cradling me against his hardness, then laid me down gently, on the bed.

He gathered my dress up and over my head, his gaze lingered on my body for a maddening amount of time before he slowly bowed and brushed my skin with his lips. A look of desire passed over his face when he looked up at me. He traced his fingertips so lightly over my underwear, then made quick work of removing them.

My skin crawled with goosebumps as he slipped out of his clothes. He put a knee down on the bed, sliding beside me, and pulled a fluffy white duvet up around us.

He pulled me to him, locking his arms around me. "Are you all right, Frankie?"

Staring into his green eyes, I nodded, then lifted my head to find his lips. The kiss was long, gentle. Sweet. I didn't know what to expect, in Michael's bed, but it definitely wasn't a deep, tender kiss, especially after how fast clothes came off.

At some point, the kiss turned me frantic, pulling at his hair, letting my nails sink into his back.

He matched my urgency for a while before tearing his mouth away from mine. Not ready for the kiss to end, I started to protest. I let out a tortured gasp as he took forever to kiss down my clavicle, between my breasts and further.

"Oh."

His tongue traced up and down, but he didn't linger. His hand slid further down. "You're already ready for me," he whispered.

Thousands of sensations whirred through my body, but somehow I managed to squeak out, "Is that bad?"

His free hand combed through my hair. "No. It's perfect. You want this as bad as I do."

He climbed up over me, spreading my legs gently, settling between them. His lips flicked against mine, and our eyes locked.

I felt the pressure of his cock, near my opening. I took a shuddering breath of anticipation, and he sank into me, slowly, inch by delicious inch. When he was fully inside, he stayed there, still, our hearts thundering together. I'd never felt so connected to anyone in all my life.

"Oh," I sighed and cupped his face with my hand. "Michael."

His arms slid tightly under me, pulling me closer to him. He moved, slowly and gently inside of me, keeping me cradled to him and occasionally peppering my face with kisses. He was distracting, with his delicious smell, his hard perfection, completely mangling my senses. Plus, this was Michael, the Michael, who I'd known forever, on top of me, *inside* me. That alone was enough to fuck with my mind.

But eventually, feeling won out over sanity. I found myself throwing caution to the wind. I wanted more, I wanted much more. He matched my pace with his thrusts. I pressed a hand onto his chest, moving him away from me slightly to improve his angle. That's where I wanted him to be, and he let *me* decide the rhythm.

So when he erupted inside of me, I was already coming.

And coming. And coming. He kept up with my orgasm until I was finished.

I'd never had an orgasm like that. One that shook the walls, felt like it would never end. And fucking hell.

I already wanted to do it again.

EIGHTEEN

In the morning, I awoke to Saucy licking my nose, in that terribly small bed in that terribly coffin-like room … and smiled from ear to ear.

I was tucked into the crook of Michael's arm, and he was sleeping, a strange, satisfied smile on his face. The thought that I was the one who put the smile there gave me happy chills. And he was so handsome, with a rugged five o'clock shadow, hair mussed, his tanned skin contrasted against my own and the white sheets. I couldn't stop staring at him, trying to remember the first time I'd met him. Had he always been this attractive?

Alex is going to hate me—sleeping with his best friend. But it serves him right for keeping us apart for so many years.

As I rolled over and found my discarded halter dress, slipping it on, I decided that all those obstacles were now a thing of the past. They were only obstacles if I allowed them to be. Everything was finally heading in the right direction. As I shimmied into my knickers, he rolled over and looked at me. "Escaping without saying goodbye?"

"Of course not! I just thought I should head downstairs with Saucy and get us coffee."

He yawned, then reached over to grab me back onto the bed. I resisted for less than a second before falling back into his arms. "You know. Room service works down here, too."

"It does?" I chimed.

"Yes, even we Serfs have the privilege. But maybe you'd want to eat it upstairs, on your balcony?"

I leaned in and lightly kissed his lips. "I'm okay, eating it right here, in bed."

"Now you're talking." He pulled the room service menu off the table next to him and we studied it together. "One of everything?"

We had worked up an appetite, but as comfortable as I was around Michael, I still wasn't ready to pig out around him. I picked up the phone and ordered the fruit cup for me, a full big man breakfast with pancakes, eggs and sausage for Michael.

When I hung up, I rolled over onto my stomach next to him and lifted myself up on my elbows. I grinned like I knew a secret. "I've got news."

"Good news?"

I nodded, bursting with excitement.

He absently ran a finger up my bare arm, to my shoulder, and lazily coiled a lock of my hair around it. "Why didn't you tell me before?"

"Because I was a bit preoccupied," I said quickly. I probably should've prolonged the suspense, but I was practically bursting with the news. "But you know that article you said I should write, about the trip to the Everglades from a Brit's perspective?"

"Of course."

"I wrote it."

"You did?"

I nodded. "But it gets even better. I left it in Gillian's in tray yesterday morning, and that afternoon she came to me and said she wanted to publish it!"

I could tell he was pleased for me, though he didn't jump up and down like an idiot, like I'd wanted to do when I'd heard the news. He said, "Well, of course they do," as if it was destined to happen. "That's fantastic, Frankie."

"It's going to be in their next issue. But it gets even better."

"Is that right?" He seemed more interested in my arm. He'd stopped coiling my hair around the finger and now was back to rubbing my skin there, very gently almost tickling, as if trying to elicit some reaction from me. "Tell me."

"They invited me into a closed editorial meeting, and they're going to want more pieces from me. I think that means I might even have my own column soon! Just imagine—*Miami Scene, A Brit in Miami, by Francesca Benowitz*. I never had anything like that in *Slip*. Can you believe it?"

He nodded. "Absolutely. I knew you would get there."

I tilted my head. "You don't seem surprised."

"Because I knew you would, all along. I'm wondering when you're going to believe it. You're a great writer. Of course they want you."

I nudged him. "Aw. You're such a great cheerleader."

"I'm just telling the truth," he said, still stroking my arm. "So you're happy?"

"Ecstatic is more like it."

He rolled over, checking the time on the bedside alarm clock. "I'd better get in the shower. I have to be at work at nine."

Oh. Right. Work. I did, too. A day after my great big news, I'd nearly forgotten. So much had happened in such a short time.

"And before you go worrying about me, they do equip the Serf rooms with a bucket and flannel for tending to our abluting needs."

I grabbed a pillow and threw it at him. He caught it. "Do you really think I'm that spoiled?"

"No. I think what Alex told me. You're sheltered. When you were younger, your parents took care of everything for you. And then when Piers came along, you let him make all the decisions, too. A shame because in that space between you were a different person. You didn't let anyone tell you what to think. Remember?"

I shook my head. It hadn't been long but, yes, I was opinionated and sure of myself, and I'd written some wonderful pieces for the campus newspaper that had got me a fair amount of attention. I could barely remember a time when I wasn't under Piers' thumb. "Oh ... I interned a few summers at the firm. Is that what you're talking about?"

He nodded. "And no one could shut you up. You told me you were going to write a bestselling book, one day. And I believed you'd do it. You convinced us all."

169

"Well ... we're all a bit silly and idealistic when we're that age."

"No. I don't think that Frankie's gone," he said, sitting up in the bed so the sheet fell to his waist. I glanced at his muscles I'd grown acquainted with last night. "I think she's there. She needs someone to brush the dust off. That's all."

Who was this man, talking about me like I was someone who mattered? The feeling was so foreign. I smiled at him, then leaned over to kiss him. "You're a very sweet man."

"Just telling the truth."

I stood up as someone called "room service" through the door. "I suppose I should take my breakfast to go. Otherwise, I'll be late."

He nodded. "What if we eat dinner tonight ... on your balcony, this time?"

A day ago, that would've been my worst nightmare. But now, I couldn't wait. It wasn't much of a risk, considering the reward.

NINETEEN

I was bouncing off the walls by the time I made it into the *Miami Scene* offices, and it had nothing to do with the prospect of sorting projects at my computer. No, I had sex, and Michael, and every last inch of his perfect body on the brain, and I was pretty sure it'd have me cocking up my work big-time.

But I didn't care.

I'd had sex. Good sex. Sex that made me feel like my body was actually working right, and not some hopelessly malfunctioning bit of machinery that constantly needed working on. I was giddy with excitement for our date that night. I kept sniffing my cardigan because I'd worn it last night, and it smelled like his woodsy citrus aftershave.

"Well, aren't you *glowing*," Tori remarked as I sat at my desk, staring into space, dreaming of the way Michael had kissed me.

I grinned. "Oh, I just had a really nice night last night. Michael."

Tori's jaw dropped. "You're so lucky. That British fox is so dreamy," she said, but then she frowned. "Although, while that British accent is sexy to us American girls, I guess it's normal to you?"

I laughed. "Oh, no, it depends on which British man it's attached to. Michael's voice is sexy to me, too, but mostly because he is." I shivered at the thought of it. "We're seeing each other tonight, too."

Which reminded me, I needed to text Jessica. She'd go bonkers, considering she'd been after me to have sex and move on from Piers for, oh, about forever.

Which further reminded me … I hadn't thought of Piers for a full twelve hours, ever since I'd ended the call with him, the night before. That had to be a record.

"You're having such a good streak of luck," Tori said with a cautious smile. "I hope it doesn't end now. Gillian sent me over to ask you to come to her office."

My smile fell. I popped up and glanced over the cubicle wall, at the door to her office. "What? What does she want?"

She shrugged. "She asked me to send you in. But she seems to be in an okay mood."

I winced as I grabbed my pad and pen. "I'll tell you more about last night later? Girls' lunch at the taco place? If I survive?"

"Sounds good!" She followed me out to the aisle and whispered, "Good luck!"

I'd been so excited about my new editorial duties, and a little freaked by Dane's proposition, that I'd probably messed up something with my clicking-and-sorting job. But before I knocked on Gillian's office door, I'd decided that nothing would get me down. I was too high to let anything put me in a bad mood.

When I got there, the door was open, and Gillian was

talking on the phone, in her brusque, take-no-prisoners voice. I could tell it was with the advertising department, because she said, "I don't care if Tommy Bahama wants the back page. It's always belonged to Chanel. Tell them to go to hell."

She looked up and waved me in. I scooted to the chair opposite her desk and sat on the very edge of it, looking around. She may have been a woman, but she didn't have the normal womanly trappings that I saw on the desks of my female co-workers—photographs of family, proudly displayed artwork from her children, inspirational posters, homey décor and houseplants hoping to make the place look more inviting. Gillian's office was about as impersonal as an office could get. It looked more like a prison cell.

"I don't care! Tell them it's final!" she shouted into the phone. Then she slammed the receiver down in its cradle.

I had the momentary urge to sneak out and run away. This was Gillian's "okay" mood?

But when she looked up at me, her rage dissipated, and she even smiled. "Hi, Frankie. How are you?"

"Good. Tori said you wanted to see me?"

She nodded. "I was wondering what you had up your sleeve for the March issue."

It took me a moment to realise what she was asking for. That's right. My *series*. I was actually writing a series for *Miami Scene* magazine. For a moment, I imagined having my photograph in the magazine, maybe even my own section in the back, right next to the Chanel ad. Maybe people on the street would recognise me as "that quirky Brit who wrote those cheeky columns." The thought sent a thrill up my spine.

"Oh, I … I … I have a few ideas floating around," I started. I'd had a few half-formed ideas, nothing concrete. Most of it involved me, traipsing around Miami, hand in hand with Michael, giving each other googly-eyed looks, feeding each other empanadas, or something. "Is there something in particular you wanted to see?"

She nodded. "Yes. Haulover beach."

"A beach?" I smiled. "I was actually planning to do that. Is that a good one?"

"Yes. Very good." She smiled. "Of course, we'll pay for any incidentals. Just keep your receipts."

That filled me with more excitement. After much deliberation, I had bought the perfect bikini, and couldn't wait to use it. Now I had a reason. And a trip to the beach when I should be working … what could be better? "All right. Haulover beach it is, then! Is there a deadline?"

"I'd like to have it by next week. We got your first one in, just under the wire."

I nearly choked. That was soon. But how could I complain about a free beach day? Even if I'd be working all weekend to write the article, it would be worth it. "No problem at all."

"Perfect. It's not going to interfere with your interning duties, is it? We can't have anything falling through the cracks there, like last time."

She'd never let me live that down, would she? I shook my

head. It was the truth. The *article* probably wouldn't get in the way, but other things, such as the thought of Michael's glorious naked body, might. "Oh, no. No, of course not."

"Good," she said, going back to her computer. She typed something and then looked up as if surprised to see me there. "You can go."

"Thanks!" I said brightly, escaping as quickly as I could, before her mood could change again. I practically skipped back to my cubicle. I'd more than survived. And now I had an assignment for my next article. I gave Tori a thumbs-up as I passed her.

Then I quickly texted Jessica. *Guess who got laid last night?*

Jessica: Kim Kardashian?

Frankie: Funny. I know you'll never believe it, but … me.

Jessica: By yourself?

Frankie: Ha ha. No, this one involved Michael.

Jessica: ???!!!! From New Year?

Frankie: The same. Not to mention that Piers called and I hung up on him.

Jessica: !!!! CALL ME.

Frankie: I'm at work but I'll call and give you details later.

Jessica: YOU MUST. But not at 3 AM. Actually, 3 AM is fine. CALL ME!

I grinned, set my phone down, and started happily click-click-clicking on the mountain of projects that needed sorting. For the first time, the job barely bothered me, because I had something amazing to look forward to.

• • •

The giddiness still hadn't worn off by that evening. I danced into the elevator at the Four Seasons, thinking about what I should wear for my "date" with Michael. By the time I got to the door of my suite, I'd mentally selected my long, pink sundress with the spaghetti straps. I smiled at the Post-it he'd left. *Hi, beautiful. Have a late meeting. I'll pop back up at around 8.*

Good. He was thinking about me, too.

Saucy yipped excitedly as I stepped inside. I pulled him into my arms and kissed him. "We're going to have a guest, baby! So we have to look our best!"

I walked Saucy, took a shower and dressed, taking extra care, but my heart was pumping in my chest the whole time and my body was flushed with anticipation. My complexion was finally turning brown. When I finished wrestling with the curling tongs and getting my hair just so, I went to the door to the balcony and looked out.

The balcony to my room, obviously, was much bigger than his, not only with chairs but several long loungers and a patio table situated right by the railing. Even though I'd been proven wrong and we hadn't plummeted to our deaths last night, it still filled me with apprehension. But that was okay. Michael would make it better, he had before. It seemed like when he was around, everything else went away, and I could only concentrate on him.

I shivered. There was a time I'd felt the same about Piers. Was I getting obsessed, this early in our relationship? That wasn't healthy. I needed to tone it down, take it easy, not jump on him the moment he came through the door.

Taking a deep breath, I looked up and noticed the clouds, multiplying in the sky. The sun disappeared, and it was suddenly black as night. A jagged edge of lightning slit the sky, and a boom of thunder came right after that.

I blinked once, and in that split second, the skies opened up to the most awe-inspiring downpour I'd ever seen. Everything went hazy, lost in a murky miasma. The windows fogged over as things began to ping off the wooden surface of the deck outside. I realised they were golf ball-sized chunks of hail.

As I was hugging myself, wondering if this would delay Michael, there came a knock at the door. I opened it to find a drowned rat—no, more specifically, it was Michael. His once-dapper three-piece suit glued to him like a second skin and dark tubes of hair matted against his forehead. He had a five o'clock shadow and his brown skin glistened.

Before I could open my mouth to ask if he needed a towel, he shoved aside his curtain of hair and said, "My day was brilliant. How was yours?"

I burst out laughing. "Oh, hunky dory, but not as good as yours, I see."

Water dripped off the edge of his nose. "You mind if I—" He motioned inside.

"No. No, not at all." I moved aside to let him in. Saucy inspected him and started to lick the water from his shoes. "Can I get you a towel?"

He dropped his briefcase in the foyer area, shrugged

off his soaked jacket, and loosened his tie, then crouched to pet Saucy.

"Sorry about—" He motioned to himself. "All this. Would've stopped at my room but then I'd have been late."

I looked at the clock over the door. Sure enough, it was *exactly* eight o'clock. "Oh, well … I didn't order any food because I didn't know what you'd like."

He cocked a thick eyebrow at me. "Fuck the food. I didn't want to leave *you* wondering, Frankie."

Piers would never have done that. He'd come home hours late, sometimes, when I was near mad with worry, and act like *I* was the problem. Then he'd complain that the food was cold. "Oh."

Michael scanned his surroundings as he undid the buttons on his shirt, then whistled. "No wonder you looked at my room like it was a dungeon. This is very up-market." He started to pull off his shirt, leaving me gazing open-mouthed and speechless at his broad shoulders. "Can I use your shower?"

"Oh, yes." I started to walk past him. "I'll show you. It's—"

Right then he grabbed my wrist, pulling me flush against him, breathless. He was damp, but his skin was still warmer than mine. He kissed my lips, very gently. "You look gorgeous, Frankie. And how was your day?"

I nodded, stunned, speechless by his … everything. Sensation overload.

When he released me, I followed him through to the bedroom, then pointed to the master bath. "There,"

I finally rasped out like a babe speaking her first word, immediately feeling foolish. *Say something that isn't completely obvious, why don't you, Frankie?*

"Thank you," he said, shrugging off his shirt. But he wasn't looking at the bathroom. He was looking at me. In fact, we were both standing there, drinking one another in, right in front of the bed.

And god, he looked good enough to dive into and drown there. Chiselled chest, flat board of a stomach, perfect V of muscle, tapering to his waist. People sculpted and elevated to godliness forms that were far less perfect.

I stood there wondering what I should do with all of this wonder before me.

I wanted to kiss every inch of his skin, sampling every bit of the buffet before me. But was I even worthy? He was so beautiful. I was soft and squishy compared to his hard, rigid muscles. It was obvious why I was drooling, but I couldn't understand why he looked like he wanted me so much.

I lost my nerve first and looked away. "You take your shower. Then we can eat dinner. What are you in the mood—"

He grabbed my hand and closed the gap between us in one swift movement, pressing me up against the wall, his erection hard and insistent on my hip. "What if I'm not hungry for food?"

"I—" My knees weakened as his dark gaze penetrated me. "What are you hungry for?"

"Frankie." His finger grazed down my side, and I

tingled from head to toe. His breath was warm on my face. "I think you know. I've been thinking about you all day, and I can't help it. I want you now."

I have been too, I thought, but I knew saying the words would mean more time before his lips were on mine. So I kept silent, my lips quivering to taste his.

He grabbed my wrists and pinned them above my head with one hand. A low growl ripped out of his throat as he took my mouth for a commanding kiss. He tasted like coffee and sweetness, a uniquely Michael taste I couldn't seem to get enough of. I twined my fingers in his wet hair and kissed him deeper. He made another sound deep in his throat and his free hand found its way up my dress and between my legs, cupping my wet heat. I shuddered when his palm found the right place and he began edging me into excitement. His tongue pushed forward, prying my lips apart, penetrating me the way his gaze had.

The way I knew his cock soon would.

We eventually left the wall and made our way to the bed, after he'd brought me to orgasm with just his palm. I sat up on my elbows, and the loose straps on my dress slipped from my shoulders. He helped the rest of it down, undressing me slowly, as if unwrapping a particularly valuable present. When I was only wearing my thong, he stood over me, gazing in appreciation. Then he hooked his fingers through the lace of my underwear and slowly dragged the fabric down, leaving me bare.

I reached up and grabbed his belt buckle, making quick work of helping him out of his trousers. I slid them down.

I was so ready, I was practically shaking as if I were the one who'd been caught in the drenching rainstorm. I was so blinded by lust at the sight of his naked body before me that I could barely see anything *but* him.

His hands grabbed for my backside and dragged my hips forward to the edge of the bed. I drew in a sharp breath as I felt the hard erection between my legs. I scrabbled at the sheets around me, fisting them in anticipation.

I hooked a leg around his waist and we groaned in unison as his cock pushed inside me.

I knew I was ready, but I had no idea how ready I truly was. My body felt out of control and in a rush of pleasure I began to come again. He kept thrusting, his open mouth nipping at my neck, my chin, my lips.

"Frankie." His voice was rough, but still just a whisper. He kept saying my name, over and over. "Oh, fuck, Frankie."

I could only moan in answer, mostly because I didn't just forget his name. I forgot everything. This was a holy experience, reducing me to a blubbering pile of jelly. I felt a new orgasm approaching on the heels of the last one, following every single one of his thrusts as he rocked his hips into me.

After a particular terrible first time with Piers—my first time with anyone, really- he'd said the next time would be better. And it had been. But compared to this?

That was nothing. The pleasure Michael had just given me was beyond anything I'd ever experienced. I didn't even know I could have multiple orgasms.

I demanded he not stop. His eyes were clouded with heat and lust and he growled out. It jarred me because Michael was the quiet and confident type. I didn't realise he could be so loud and animalistic. My body shuddered in waves, and his arms tightened around me. He thrust harder and harder, gripping me in his solid arms. I could feel his excitement as he sped up until he finally shot deep within me.

He tore himself from me and rolled over onto the bed, his chest rising and falling, letting out another, animal-like growl.

Then, smiling, he looked over at me and kissed my shoulder. He pulled me to his chest. I didn't know a man could be so masculine and sexy and yet sweet and caring at the same time. "Now, about dinner—"

I laughed, my voice low and self-assured and decidedly unlike me. Had I really spent hours getting ready just to be ravished by him in the first five minutes? Yes, *yes*, and I didn't care. It was so worth it. "Shower?"

He chuckled. "After we eat, sweetheart. You need to keep your strength up for what I have planned for you. And I'm *starving*."

TWENTY

It turned out that having a strong, trustworthy man by my side calmed my fear of heights enormously, even while eating on the balcony of a skyscraper.

The entire night had been like a dream, as had the interceding few days. Those days had consisted of me, going to the dreary world of work and pushing papers, all the while thinking of some romantic thing Michael had done and shivering with anticipation for more. After the blur of work, I'd practically race back to the hotel, only to find him, as excited as I was. Once, he'd been outside my door with flowers. Another time, it was Thai food. He always knew exactly what I liked, in and out of bed.

So it wasn't a surprise that he was all for helping me with my article during our beach trip on Saturday. In fact, he'd been so proud of me, he called my father to tell him he was taking the day off. "It shows how special you are," he'd said. "And a special girl needs special, undivided attention. You have me for the whole day, sweetheart."

It began perfectly. We slept in, and in the morning he greeted me with strong coffee and fresh-baked croissants from the bakery across the street. We'd had a leisurely breakfast out on the balcony—by now, I loved the feeling of the morning sun on my face as I ate breakfast—and we hopped into his convertible and headed to the beach, a little before noon.

"Where is this place?" he asked from behind his mirrored sunglasses as he cruised out over the bridge on 195, toward the shore.

I checked the GPS on my phone. "It says to go north on A1A."

"And Gillian thinks this is the best beach?" he asked doubtfully.

I nodded, though as we neared the coast and the ocean broke through the palm trees, I saw plenty of white sand and bronzed bodies. There were so many people out there already, the women in obscenely small bikinis, soaking up the sun. Where Piers would've been side-eyeing them all beneath his dark shades, Michael, though, seemed disinterested in everyone there. Even though in my bikini, I wasn't a supermodel, and my weeks in Miami hadn't made me much darker than the colour of dough, I didn't care. Michael snaked his hand over the gearstick then rested it possessively on my thigh, his fingers running circles on my skin. If Michael liked who I was, who cared?

Secure in that thought, I smiled brightly as Michael found A1A and we headed north, the white stretches of sand on my right. I grabbed my sunscreen and started to apply it to my face and arms. "That's some bikini," he said, glancing at my body. "Where'd you get it?"

I basked in the compliment, adjusting the matching see-through cover-up. "Here in Miami, at a boutique. They have the greatest bikinis in this town. I've never actually worn one, but I figured, when in Rome!"

"Good choice. You look stunning." He smirked and reached for one of the side ties on the bottoms. "I think my favourite thing about it is going to be taking it off you, later."

I couldn't help it. I giggled. Then I glanced up from squeezing a glob of sunscreen into my palm and saw the sign. "Oh. Here it is. Haulover Park." I motioned to an open spot on the side of the road. "Park here."

He pulled into the spot and removed his sunglasses. "Uh ... Frankie?"

I'd been busy, trying to lather the sunscreen on my chest. I didn't want a repeat of our first date together. "What? You might need to get the places I can't reach. Like my back?"

"Frankie?" He sounded more concerned now.

I looked at him and realised he'd gone a bit pallid. His dark skin looked greenish. "Are you all right?"

I followed his line of sight toward two women, walking hand in hand through the beach entrance.

They were stark naked.

My jaw dropped, but unfortunately, that wasn't the most shocking thing out there. What was even more shocking was that these two women were not alone. Everyone—young and old—was absolutely without a stitch of clothing.

"You're going to need more sunscreen," Michael remarked.

I gawked at the scene before me. I tried to avert my eyes, but everywhere they went held another thing I shouldn't be looking at. Naked men playing football, their little cocks wagging with the exertion. Naked women sitting on beach chairs, eating peaches, the juice dripping on their tanned breasts. A naked lifeguard, wearing nothing but a whistle, around his neck. "This has to be the wrong place?"

But no, this was Haulover Beach. The beach Gillian had specifically wanted me to write about.

Now, thinking back to the expression on her face, with an amusement that had puzzled me, it fell into place—she'd been *hoping* to get this kind of reaction from me. Nice one, really.

I thought we'd zoom off, go somewhere else. But Michael pulled off his seatbelt and quickly hopped out. "Come on," he said, opening my door.

I stared at him, incredulous. "We're not ... going *there*?"

"Well, yeah. You have to write about it, don't you?"

"Yes, but—" I'd heard Americans were prudish about showing off their bodies; Europeans were far more blasé about these things. But *I* had never done anything like this before.

"You sure?" He looked around and shrugged. "There are a few people wearing clothes. You don't have to strip. We can stay long enough to get the material for your article, and then we'll go. Fifteen minutes?"

That didn't sound so bad. I struggled to my feet and noticed he was right. There were a few people in clothes, though my eyes didn't seem to want to behave and look at them. They wandered to the old man with the monstrous fifth appendage, who was walking toward me with a proud swagger. My gaze darted from the ground to the sky, skirting around everyone's midriffs.

Michael went to the trunk and got the beach chairs and umbrella he'd rented as I stood there, awkwardly studying my pedicure. Minutes ago, I'd been feeling so free, so comfortable in my skin, and now, I felt off-kilter again, like a turtle retreating into her shell. I followed behind Michael, head down, like a misbehaving child. If Michael was uncomfortable, though, you wouldn't know it. He was as calm and collected as ever as he marched us onto the beach and set up our chairs. He even bought two iced teas from a naked vendor for us, without batting an eye.

When he'd set up our chairs, I scuttled into it, under the shade, put my sunglasses on, and sat slumped and hugging myself, staring straight at the empty expanse of ocean in front of me. Thankfully, there were no naked swimmers out there. *Fifteen minutes. Fifteen minutes, and we are out of here.*

"You can at least try to enjoy yourself," Michael murmured to me, and I could sense a smile in his voice. "It's a new experience. I bet it's very freeing."

I couldn't imagine that. "I'm not having anyone else look at my goodies, thank you."

"Actually, I hear, in places like this, you kind of learn to ignore it. You get used to it."

I turned, jaw dropped in shock, and inspected him

over the tops of my sunglasses. "Michael Evans. Are you telling me that you're actually thinking of losing those trunks?"

He shrugged. "Well … Like you said. When in Rome."

I gasped. "You wouldn't."

But I didn't know. All these years, Michael had always struck me as one of the most upstanding, straight-laced types. He was careful, conservative. Ruffled no feathers. And *then*, I'd got into bed with him. And I'd realised everything I thought I knew about Michael was only on the surface. There was so much more to him, and it intrigued me.

"I might." He smiled. "If you do."

I hugged myself tighter. "No. No, no, no. No."

He shrugged. "Okay. Might be freeing. That's all. And it's not like you know anyone here. And you know, to get the *full experience*, for your article—"

I pressed my lips together, considering this. He maybe had a point. It wasn't *just* about getting the goods for my article. No, Piers always wanted me covered up. I'd been living in his cage for far too long. I'd made so many strides over the past few months to get away from him, but there was always more I could do. And what better way to say a proverbial "eff you" to him?

Quickly, I sat up in the beach chair and pulled off my cover-up. Then I untied the top of my bikini and let everything hang out. Warm air kissed places that had never seen the outside world before, and I shivered a little, but did my best to keep my shoulders back, and head high.

"I know you wanted to be the one to take this off me," I said, slipping the rest of it off and setting it aside, "But—"

"That's okay," he said with a grin, lifting his butt and pulling off his trunks. "I'll deal with that later," he said, eyeing up what I had just uncovered. He reached over and grabbed my hand, and we sat there, sipping iced tea and having a lovely time.

So lovely, in fact, that we didn't leave until dinnertime.

TWENTY-ONE

"I'm exhausted!" I said. It was growing dark when we arrived at the hotel. We'd had dinner and mojitos at a place on the strip, and after all that sun and sea air, I felt sleepy and a little woozy. There was still sand and salt on my skin, and a little burn, too, but I was happier and more satisfied than I'd ever been. I'd even composed the first few lines of my article in my head, on the drive back. "I just want to take a shower and go to sleep."

"All right, sweetheart," he said, squeezing my hand. "I'll run the water for you and get you tucked in."

But then our eyes locked, and that was all it took to make my stomach clench. I scraped my top teeth over my bottom lip, thinking that sleep wasn't the answer. No, I'd spent a lot of the day staring at his naked body and getting randy. What I needed most was more of that magic touch of his.

I asked, "Would you take a shower with me?"

His eyes flashed to mine. The speed with which he came to my side was Olympic. He started to usher me down the hall, but we didn't get very far. Before I could reach the doorknob, his hands were on me, gripping me possessively. He whirled me to him in the narrow hallway, clamped his hands around my body, and slammed his hard body against mine. His mouth settled on mine, and I surrendered myself to him. Right at that moment, I knew I would stay there and let him do whatever he pleased. I'd let him claim whatever he wanted … and I'd love it.

He kissed me again unlike the Michael I knew, fucking my mouth with his tongue, his big hand engulfing my throat, then sliding down over my breasts. He reached the bottom hem of my camisole and slid his hand inside, cupping my breast and running his fingers over my nipple as I desperately pushed my tongue into his mouth. His other hand came around my neck, pulling the tie from my ponytail. My hair spilled down my shoulders as I pressed myself up against him.

Lifting my ass and pressing me against the wall, he broke the kiss and dragged his mouth, rough and wet, over my chin, down my throat to my breastbone. His teeth caught the fabric of my suit and he lifted it down over my nipple.

I growled. Somewhere in the back of my mind, I knew we were treading dangerous territory. It felt like he was on his way to becoming my whole universe, like I'd just gone from one man to the next, and maybe I should slow down. I tried to remain still, in breathless anticipation of what he'd do, where his mouth and hands would move next, because I wanted to remember this, to remember the path his fingers and tongue trailed over every single part of my flesh.

But I was already close to losing my mind and forgetting myself completely.

"Please," I moaned as he freed both my breasts from my bikini and continued to lavish his attention on them. He carried me into the bathroom. I wound my hands around the nape of his neck as he manoeuvered to open the door of the shower stall and twisted the shower knob. Thick, hot steam filled the air creating a veil of haze between us. He began to kick off his shoes, staring intently into my eyes, his forehead pressed against mine.

He felt the temperature of the water, never letting me go. That was how strong and amazing he was; he kept me cradled in his arms like he didn't want to lose one minute of his skin against mine. "You like it hot?"

I nodded, knowing it was about to get hotter.

We tore at our remaining clothes until we were, for the most part, naked. Then stepped into the spacious glass shower nook. Steam filled the room casting us in a dream-like, fantasy world as he caged me within his impressively muscular frame and his mouth descended on mine in a plundering, ravishing kiss. Desire flickered through me as he swept down, covering my breast with his mouth, fiercer than ever.

"I love your breasts, Frankie," he murmured, biting one with his teeth until I cried out. "I've been wanting to do this all day."

I arched my spine as he squeezed the flesh and sucked it to a hardened point. I tilted my head up and let the water pound on my face, watching as the drops fell upon the magnificent, tan skin of his shoulders. I fisted his hair in my hands and leaned into him.

He licked his way up the hollow of my throat, to the tip of my chin. He nibbled and bit at my lips, one hand grasping my hair as the other slipped between my legs. He rubbed the pad of his finger there and I squirmed against him. Tendrils of sensation lit everywhere in my body as I raked my hands down his strong back, feeling the coiled tension in his shoulders as he rubbed me, slowly, gently, maddeningly, with his fingers.

"Take me," I whispered against his damp skin, scenting him, wanting all my senses to drown in him. "Just take me now, right here."

"Whatever you say," he said, dipping his head and kissing the shell of my ear.

The pleasure was immediate and intense. *How could someone so easily make you feel like this*? Michael was teaching me something very valuable; chemistry and mutual desire were a real turn on. Once again, he primed me so easily that I was almost embarrassed at how fast I succumbed. He didn't do anything more than brush against my sex, alternating firm pressure with whipping, feather-light touches. He could tell by my moans that I liked what he was doing. He took advantage of my moans, reading my body like a book and pleasuring me more. I ran my hands down the smooth contours of his chest, my insides clenching, tightening, exploding with so much pressure that I gasped out, falling against him. The orgasm was electric, bolts of lightning zapping straight to my toes.

"Michael—" I could barely stand. I slumped into him,

wobbling. He made my orgasms so deliciously intense like heaven and earth were moving around us.

He put a finger on my lip, quieting me. I was shuddering still, muscles slowly relaxing, turning to that great big pile of useless jelly that his intense orgasms made me.

He guided me under the stream of warm water and became my nursemaid. Running his big hands down my hair, spilling sweet-smelling shampoo into his palm and lathering into my scalp. I felt so relaxed and pampered that I never wanted to move out of this shower nook. I let the water rinse away the suds as he went for a bar of soap. I closed my eyes and felt his hands rubbing everywhere, making me breathless from the contact.

He lifted my arms one at a time and slid the soap in long soothing motions. He continued between my legs, working methodically. His body bulged in all the right places, his torso glistening and wet, his nipples erect with excitement, his glorious cock hard and ready while he worked on me. It excited me to see him this aroused and still focused on me. I felt my mouth salivating for him, but when I tried to touch, he nudged my hands away. He lathered himself quickly, and I helped him, working my hands over his body.

I wasn't sure of this feeling, because I'd never felt it before.

But it felt like he was worshipping me. Taking care of me.

And right then, I decided there was no such thing as falling too fast. Not when you know you're landing in a place where hurt isn't possible.

TWENTY-TWO

In the hours after Michael left me alone to get some work done, I wrote long into the night, and when I was done I felt like this article was even better than my last. It was witty and honest and everything I'd hoped it would be when I'd sat down in front of the blank computer screen. The words had flown from my fingertips again, as if Michael had instilled some magic within me that tapped into my talent. I'd had no idea, then, but when I was with Piers, that part of me had been stifled, caged. And now, I could only let it out as fast as my fingers could fly across the keyboard.

After a quick proofread, I sent it off to Gillian, not even questioning that she would adore it. It was everything *Miami Scene* wanted. Since when had I ever felt that about my writing? Even at *Slip*, I'd been constantly second-guessing my articles, reading them over and over again before submitting, expecting to be sacked as a talentless hack at any moment, despite the effusive praise that always followed. Now, it was like I owned my abilities. *I* valued them. I valued *myself*.

Even though it was after two and I had to get back to work early in the morning, I was wide awake. Stroking

Saucy on my lap, I thought about taking a shower, but then I sniffed my skin. It smelled like him. No, I'd wait a little longer.

Instead, I called Jessica. It was a weekday, so I knew she'd be up, appropriately caffeinated and getting ready for work. She might've played hard, but she worked hard, too, which meant early gym mornings and office hours, even when she'd spent all night hard-drinking at a club. I'd never known a woman to bounce back from a drinking binge faster than Jessica—the word hangover simply wasn't in her vocabulary.

"Tell me everything," she said immediately, though her voice was far away, with a slight echo. I must've been on speaker. I heard the clacking of a hair tool, probably her curling wand. "But why are you up so late? Is everything okay?"

"Oh. It's more than okay," I gushed dreamily.

A pause. "Let me guess. Michael?"

My heart fluttered at the name, spoken aloud. I had to repeat it. "Michael."

"What's that mean? Have you been stuffed?"

I grinned so wide I thought my face might break. "Have I ... goodness. You'd be so proud of me, Jess. I almost feel like I'm living in a porn film."

I expected her to be thrilled. After all, sex was top on Jessica's list. And she was the one who'd wanted me to have a meaningless shag to put distance between me and Piers. This should have delighted her. Instead, she said, "Hmm."

"What is that supposed to mean?"

"What I mean is that it happened very fast."

I snorted. "You shag most guys on the first date."

"The first *hour*," she corrected.

She seemed rather proud of the fact.

"So what's wrong with Michael?"

"Well, it's not that he isn't scrummy, but he's also so … close to you. Your father's employee. Your brother's friend, isn't he? I mean, he's a lot more entangled in your life than Piers ever was. If he breaks your heart—"

"Oh, he won't," I said assuredly.

"But if he *does* … oh, bugger!" She let out a string of curses. "I poked my eyeball with the bloody mascara wand. Oh, I'm going blind!"

She let out some more screams, ever the drama queen, and suddenly, I didn't want to be on the phone anymore. I'd expected a far different reaction than the one I'd got from my best friend. She actually sounded disappointed in me. "I'll let you go then."

"No. Wait, Frankie. Look. I'm happy for you, I really am. And you sound happy, which is great. But I know you. You don't like to rush into anything. You like to take your time."

"I didn't with—" I stopped. I'd begun to say, *I didn't with Piers,* but look how that had turned out. "I don't always."

"Maybe. But I'm saying that this isn't like you."

I frowned. "I don't understand. First, you want me to move on as fast as possible, and now you're unhappy that I'm moving on?"

"I'm not unhappy! I'm happy for you. I just expected that you'd play around a bit, learn to enjoy your independence, you know ... before falling into this again. This sounds so very ... serious."

"Well, I know I didn't expect it to happen. And I certainly didn't want to rush into anything so soon. But when it's right ... you know. And I know this is nothing like Piers."

"All right, darling," she said, to the sound of water running. But this sound was different. Was she ... peeing on speaker phone? Probably. I wouldn't put it past Jessica. "Keep me posted. I'm chuffed that you're happy. It's beyond brilliant. Miss you."

"Miss you, too," I said, ending the call. I let Saucy down off my lap, brought the crook of my elbow to my nose, and inhaled deeply, dragging it in like a hit of heroin.

Maybe Jessica was right. Was I becoming addicted? Would the crash be even worse than Piers?

So I went to take a shower and get ready for bed. But as I was walking to the bathroom, I noticed a text from Michael: *Tomorrow night?*

The dreamy grin returned and I threw caution to the wind.

TWENTY-THREE

Two days later, Tori was out with a virus, so I was sitting in my cubicle, enjoying my tea and finishing up my project management division for the day. As I clicked away at the screen, sorting the projects to different departments and feeling enormously zen about my life, I sensed a presence behind me.

I knew right away that it was Dane. He was the only one who came into my cubicle like a ninja. I could feel him, staring holes in my back. But as important as he *thought* he was, Dane was an inconsequential person to me; I was in too good a mood to let him nettle me.

I spun around in my chair. "Are you trying to be creepy or is there something about the back of my head that interests you?"

The smirk came back. "You have an interesting ... uh ... skull-shape, for sure," he said, his eyes moved around my work-space. "But that's not why I'm here."

I snorted. "OK."

"Just wanted to tell you ... Gillian really liked your article."

I raised an eyebrow. I *knew* that. We'd had a meeting where she practically gushed for an entire hour. So I knew he wasn't here to compliment me on that. Did he ever compliment anything that wasn't produced by his own hand?

"And?"

He checked over the cubicle, as if to see if anyone else was coming, then leaned in. "A word of advice. You're Gillian's little darling right now. Milk it. You can probably write whatever you want, and she'd let you."

Oh? Was he actually being nice? "Why do you say that?"

"Because I was there once, too. I produced a couple of great pieces—one that was even on the short-list for a bunch of awards. She was thrilled. But when she gets comfortable with you, she'll give you hell for any idea you come up with, no matter how good it is."

"Oh, but your article covering the sights and sounds of the mango festival was a masterpiece," I gushed, before I'd even realised I'd done it.

Great. Now he was going to think of me as one of his groupies. One of his eyebrows lifted in surprise, but he said, "That was a long time ago. Just giving you a word to the wise."

Truth be told, I'd read more than just that one article— they were good. Really good. The man had more talent than most of the writers at *Slip*. So, curious as to what another writing professional thought, I asked, "What did *you* think of my article?"

He shrugged. "It was decent." He grabbed the open chair beside my desk, flipped it around and straddled it, gazing into my eyes. "Would've been better with pictures, though."

I rolled my eyes. "Ha. Ha. I did take pictures. Remember?"

"Not the right ones, though."

Of course. He wanted pictures of busty women's naked bodies, which was strictly forbidden at nude beaches, not to mention, probably wouldn't have suited *Miami Scene's* family readership very well, either. The photos I'd grabbed were of the beach's entrance sign, and a few of the ocean, *sans* naked bums. "You can get plenty of that by just looking out the window. There are all kinds of women wearing the teeniest of bikinis, right out there on the strip," I reminded him.

He swept a lock of wayward hair off his forehead and fixed me with that charming gaze. "Maybe I wanted to see one in particular."

Right. The only thing a man like Dane wanted to look at was himself. It's funny to think that the first time I met him, I thought he was a complete one-eighty to Piers. But other than the scruffy appearance, he had so much in common with Piers, it was almost farcical. They were all male posturing, mere animals in the wild, trying to spread their seed as far and wide as possible.

"Thanks," I said, starting to turn back to my computer. "But the thought leaves me a little nauseated."

He reached out and caught my chair before I could turn all the way. His forearm strained to hold it back, even as I shoved. I pressed my lips together, about to tell him to go to hell, when he said, "Come on. When I asked you out before, I didn't know how much *fun* you could be. Now I really want to go out with you."

"Wait, you asked me out?" I asked, in mock confusion. "From what I seem to remember, you just wanted to fuck."

He let go of the chair's arm and held up a finger. "No. Wrong. I did tell you we should hang out first so I could give you the lay of the editorial department, tips like the one I just gave you."

"But then you were going to lay *me*."

He gave me a look that said, *Well, if the shoe fits ...* "I admit, most of my dates usually do end up with a fair amount of really good fucking."

I glared at him. "*Really good*, by whose estimation? Yours?"

A shrug. "I get no complaints."

After that, he stared at me, expectant, waiting for an answer. As if I hadn't already given him one. I carefully crossed and uncrossed my legs, then grabbed my teacup and took a demure sip. It gave me great satisfaction to make him wait since people like him clearly thought the whole world waited on them.

"You really do want me to vomit, don't you?" I said, smiling sweetly. It was so much easier to talk to a cretin like Dane when I had my own, wonderful man to come home to.

It wasn't a blow to his iron-clad ego. Not by a long shot. He slid off the chair, lifted it, and deposited it back against the wall. "Let me guess. You're still seeing someone."

202

"Right. And I know you said you wouldn't tell a soul if we fucked but, unlike you, I actually believe in truth and honesty in a relationship."

He seemed surprised by this. "Believe it or not, I'm with you. Truth and honesty rock. But it's in such short supply. Which is why I don't do relationships, so more power to you." He winked. "Who is the lucky *bloke*? The one you went to the beach with?"

I nodded. "Michael."

"Oh, right. He's the bigwig Brit I've seen Gillian meeting with, huh?"

"Yes. He consults with the company's legal counsel."

"Right. Gillian told me, he's been pretty indispensable with a few lawsuits the magazine wound up in," he said, finally moving to the exit. "Got you this job, did he?"

I blinked. "No." Well, technically, my father had, but I'd hoped that was just between him and Gillian. If it got around that I was the beneficiary of nepotism, I was afraid none of my co-workers would look at me the same again. "It turns out that pushing paper for peanuts is not actually a very in-demand job. You think I couldn't have got it on my own?"

He shrugged. "Not *that* job. The writing job. Gillian told me that your boyfriend all but threatened her that if we didn't give you a chance, he'd make things difficult for us."

My jaw dropped. I couldn't speak for at least a full ten seconds. When I did, it was barely a whisper: "What?"

He must've been looking to get a reaction from me because he smiled. "Oh. You didn't know?"

I couldn't move. My brain was going into overdrive, trying to imagine Michael, threatening anyone. He'd shown a new side to me, lately—one who was not just kind but rather adventurous, one I couldn't deny I liked. But did he have another side? A cutthroat, threatening side? He was a lawyer, after all, and being a lawyer sometimes meant busting balls. But if so, I hadn't seen it. Not in twenty years of knowing him.

Still ... I never had been a good judge of character when it came to men.

Dane scratched his neck and looked over the cubicle wall at someone, waving slightly at them. Then he said, "Well, I wouldn't worry. Like I said, even if your boyfriend got you the job, you wrote pretty decently. I don't think it'll hurt our readership that much."

Pretty decent. That was nothing like the gushing Gillian had been doing over my articles. Had Michael put her up to it? I'd been so excited to tell Michael about how they wanted me to write for the magazine, and he'd been so genuinely happy for me. Little had I known that he'd orchestrated the whole thing, dancing me around like a puppet on strings.

What a very Piers-like thing to do.

A sick feeling planted itself in my gut and started to bloom, making that prospect of vomiting suddenly very real.

"So let me know how that *truth and honesty* in your relationship works out, okay?" he said, knocking on the cubicle wall. "I'll catch you later. And remember, my offer still stands. I'd love to give you a whirl."

He sauntered off, leaving me covered in goosebumps and shaking like a leaf, and this time, it had nothing to do with the Arctic air they pumped into the office.

TWENTY-FOUR

Since arriving in Miami, I'd been growing happier and happier. I saw more of the old Francesca Benowitz coming out, the pre-Piers woman who spoke her mind, took the bull by the horns, made things happen.

But where the old Frankie would've gone livid, would've stalked to Michael's hotel room and given him a piece of her mind ... *this* Frankie, the new person I'd become with my wanker ex-fiancé's help, didn't do that. No, instead, she moped up to her room, ripped the cutesy Post-it from Michael off the door without reading it, trudged inside her flat, and climbed under the covers of her bed, hoping to die there.

I was angry, yes. But more than anything, I was ... sad. Tired. Done.

I opened my Ativan bottle and took out the last pill. I hadn't had them. Hadn't needed them. I'd met with Hargrove once, and got a prescription, but never filled it. Now, I sucked it down, knowing it wouldn't be enough. Not for all the anxiety in my chest.

There had always been parts of Piers' heart that he'd kept sheltered from me. I knew that and chose to ignore it. I thought he was allowed his secrets, and as long as he loved me, he could keep them. I'd been wrong. But *Michael*? I thought I knew every last inch of his heart. His mind. Everything. I thought I knew him inside and out, and that would protect me from falling into the same trap twice. I didn't think there was a thing he'd kept from me.

Likely, he hadn't told me he'd interfered in my life to spare my feelings. Maybe my father had told him I was having a rough go of it, and he'd done it out of charity. For my own good. But *why* he had kept it from me didn't matter. That he *had* was enough.

He'd lied.

That was the thing I'd told myself, all those tear-filled nights of kicking myself, asking myself how I could be so *stupid*. During those nights I'd never to put up with a liar again.

Piers wasn't absolute evil. If he had been, I never would've entertained the idea of marrying him. He had likely thought, at first, that he was lying for my own good, too. Maybe it'd been some small white lie about why he'd come home late for dinner. Perhaps he'd spent a few extra minutes flirting with a secretary, and decided I didn't need to know. *No use in making it into something it's not*, he'd likely thought. But as those things usually do, it had only grown. More lies, bigger lies, piling on top of one another until absolutely nothing was the truth.

And maybe this was Michael's start. Maybe it would get worse. The thought tore at me.

So no more liars. Ever again.

I climbed into bed and burrowed under the covers,

only pulling them off when Saucy yipped, wanting to snuggle with me. I reached down, scooped him up, and held him close to my heart, trying to stop the pain. That's what it was—a physical, sharp, arrow-like pain, shooting right through my heart.

The entire flat was dark when Saucy started to yip. I pulled off the covers, smoothing the static cling from my hair as I heard the knocking at the door. I sat up in bed and listened. It came again, more urgent, and then Michael's voice called: "Frankie? You in there?"

I got out and padded to the door. Saucy barked like a guard dog at my ankles. I nudged him away and stood at the door, hand on the doorknob. Saucy looked at me, wondering why I wasn't opening it.

I had a very good reason. I knew that if I looked at Michael, I'd probably cave. Even now, I craved his touch. His closeness. I'd been through that with Piers—that gnawing desire to be with someone you couldn't be with. It felt like salt in an old wound. The only way I could think to make it stop hurting would be to let him take me to bed.

"Frankie?" Michael continued to pound. He knew something was wrong. For the past few weeks, I'd come home from *Miami Scene*, regular as clockwork, only to jump in bed with him and spend the hours until morning feasting on each other.

My every pore seemed to want that to happen, again, but my brain rebelled. "Go away," I muttered.

He didn't. That only spurred him into action. He

twisted the doorknob from the other side. I knew he would, I knew I should've kept quiet, but as much as I wanted him to go away, a larger part of me wanted an explanation. Wanted him to make it better.

But could he?

"Frankie, sweetheart. What's wrong? Did something happen?"

Oh, it had. He had no idea. And I wanted him to understand how much he'd hurt me. Maybe if I'd shown it to Piers, he never would've done it to me, again. So I pulled open the door an inch and spat, "You lied to me."

He was more surprised by the way I looked than my words. I'm sure I looked hideous, mascara on my cheeks, hair a sticky mess. "Darling, I can explain-"

"You should've done that before," I snapped. "You had plenty of opportunities, Michael. It's too late now."

He dropped his chin to his chest. "I did it because I wanted the best for you, Frankie. You've got to believe that."

I did. But it didn't matter. What was I, some child who had to be guided by those who knew better than me? What a very Piers-like thing to do. "I don't want to see you here. Ever again." I wasn't going to let anyone handle my life anymore. I wanted to be in charge of my own successes and failures, whatever they may be.

I slammed the door and leaned my back against it. The exhilaration over taking control, ending things on my terms was short-lived, though. The second I looked down at Saucy and saw his rueful face, the pain in my heart intensified.

I turned and listened, hoping he'd give it another go. We'd fight, and fight and then we'd have some lovely, hot make-up sex.

But as I pressed my ear against the door, all I could hear was retreating footsteps.

He'd left me.

That easily. Too easily.

My heart twisted. Even bloody bastard *Piers* had fought harder for me.

Tears threatened to spill from my eyes, but I held them back. I'd decided long ago that I was done crying over men. I went back to the bedroom, refusing to look at the place where I'd spent far too much time, adoring Michael. Not only that, back in London, my bed had been the place I'd spent far too much time, moping.

No moping. I wasn't that Frankie anymore. Instead, I grabbed my purse and my phone. I'd get take-out. Have a little happy me-time. Do what Jessica had told me to do and enjoy my own company.

No. Even better, I'd go out. And I knew exactly who could help me with that. I fished my phone from my purse and dialled Tori.

When she answered a moment later, she sounded as though she was in a wind tunnel. I could barely hear her. "Tori?"

"Yeah. Frankie? Is that you?"

"Yes!" I said, trying to mimic her happy-go-lucky tone. I refused to be a downer tonight. "Where are you? I was wondering if you wanted to go out, have a few drinks?"

"Frankie! I'm already out!" Before I could feel disheartened, she added: "You should come out with us. It's Ladies' Night at Liv!"

"Liv? Who is th—"

"It's a club. Oh, you must come here! You'll love it. It's so posh, and we just saw Lil Wayne."

"Lil who?"

"Just come! You're going to have so much fun! I'll see you?"

"Yes. Fine," I said, hanging up the phone and gathering my courage. I'd heard the club scene in Miami was something else. No better time than now to experience it. Over the past few weeks, I'd done a little shopping and bought a few ensembles that Piers would never approve of, so I grabbed one—a black body-con dress with a cutout under the breasts, and slipped it on, along with a pair of stiletto heels. I did my make-up as dramatically as I could, as quickly as I could, dusting my eyes with smoky black powder then straightened my hair. I threw my dark red lipstick and blusher into my Chanel bag and stepped outside, ready for the night, only a half-hour later.

By then, I'd confirmed Michael was gone. He hadn't even left me another Post-it note, like he was so fond of doing. It was like he'd given up on me.

I decided I wouldn't think of him for the rest of the night, and go out and have the time of my life. Get drunk, meet men, enjoy myself … and try to forget about the pain.

TWENTY-FIVE

When I reached the lobby, my Ativan was already kicking in. I calmly asked the doorman where I could find Club Liv. He put me in a taxi, and about twenty minutes later, I stepped out on a busy sidewalk by the beach. I checked my lipstick in my compact mirror and made my way over to a building swarming with young, scantily clad women and men. I thought I looked pretty good; my long thick hair tumbled around my shoulders like a cloak, framing the dress's cut-outs'.

The bouncers welcomed me in, and I didn't have to pay a cover charge. The place was dark, with bass pounding and blinding lasers and strobe lights, with a number of sofas set around a massive dance floor and various alcoves roped off for VIPs. The main area was a dome, with a star-shaped fixture above. In the dimness, everyone looked the same—like a dark blob.

I stood there for a moment, wondering how on Earth I was going to find Tori. The moment I made up my mind to take a step toward the bar and order something to drink, a male voice said over my shoulder, "Fancy meeting you here."

I whirled and saw Dane. He was dressed casually in a

white shirt, open halfway down his chest, which was different from his normal t-shirt and jeans but accentuated his muscled, tan body just as well. *Does everyone in Miami have an amazing body?*

I couldn't hide my surprise. "Dane! What are you—"

"Same as you, I'd say." He smirked down at me, a wolfish look on his face. "So you finally decided to take a night off from the ol' ball and chain? You alone?"

"Uh, yes. I mean, no. I'm looking for Tori."

"Ah." He pointed up a set of stairs to an alcove. From there, I could see Tori's blonde head. I started to thank him and head there when he grabbed my hand. "We should dance later."

I shook my head. "Thanks. But I'll need a lot more drinks for th—" Then it hit me. Why not? After all, hadn't Jessica said that I needed to put space between myself and the betrayal? Dane was pretty much a sure thing. Not to mention, absolutely scrummy.

I looked over my shoulder to confirm the fact, and yes—*ridiculously* scrummy—and as I did, I tripped over a couple of girls heading to the loo. They, too, were watching him, a little mesmerised, as were most of the women in his orbit.

Doing my best to ignore it, I climbed the stairs to find Tori with a gaggle of other girls with long, straight hair. Together, they looked like quadruplets. "Woooooooo!" Tori screamed when she saw me, holding up her martini glass. The other girls joined in. They were already drunk.

There were already a dozen empty drink glasses on the

small table in front of them, some of which she knocked over as she skirted around it and pulled me into a hug. "You're over the virus, then?" I shouted over the music, but she was too far gone to understand what I was saying regardless of the decibel level pumping through the speakers.

"I'm so glad you came, girl! Frankie, these are my friends. Friends! Frankie." She slurred her words frightfully, yelling them over the bass, spittle flying everywhere. *"Leth getcha drink! Thee dolla martini!"*

"Wooooo!" the girls screamed, holding up their glasses. They pulled me down to the sofa and I was quickly absorbed into their drunken conversation, though little of it made sense. They had a number of eager men providing them with drinks, so a few in, I was feeling very pleasant, my worries with Michael far behind me. Sandwiched between two women with large hoop earrings and crop halter tops that bared their pierced bellies, I was perfectly happy.

Tori grabbed me for a selfie, as Dane appeared on the landing. He locked eyes with me and winked.

Suddenly, my men troubles seemed to come flooding back. As usual, the alcohol had me feeling randy. I tried to shake off the feeling by downing another martini, as Tori grabbed my hand. "I love this song! Let's dance!"

Somehow, and it was a blur by then, we wound up on the dance floor. We packed the floor, a tangle of bodies, moving to the pulsating beat. Though the girls danced in a circle, the men hovered at the edge, moving in, trying to gyrate against us. I felt a body, behind my own, hands, brushing down my sides, warm breath on my neck. He leaned in and his lips grazed my ear. "You're so sexy."

I felt sexy. I wasn't thinking, all I knew was I wanted him closer to me. I felt invincible. I didn't need Piers, or Michael or anyone to tell me that. Jessica wanted me to live life on my own? Well, here I was. I could do anything.

Even dance with a guy—hell, fuck him if I wanted to—and I would be fine.

It was only when Tori leaned in, a warning look on her face, and slurred, "Wha ya doin wihhim?" that it hit me.

I turned and realised it was Dane. He leaned in. "Want to get out of here?"

Yes. Yes, I did.

I pushed my hips up against him and my eyes trailed to Tori, who looked absolutely horrified. "Well ... it wouldn't be terrible, would it?" I asked.

She blinked. Shrugged a little. Leaned on me. I think she was having trouble staying on her feet. "Dunno."

He had his hands on my waist and was nuzzling my neck. I smelled his cologne, the alcohol on his breath, felt the stubble on his chin brushing my throat, and my insides did a dance of excitement. Tori grinned. "Whatevs, go for it! Buwhuddabout your British bloke?" She actually spit on me with the last word.

I shook my head. "He's ... it's complicated. He's not here."

"Really?" She squinted into the distance, beyond the dance floor, shielding her eyes from the glare of the neon lights with her hand. "*Intatim*?"

Confused, it took me a moment to translate. *Isn't that him?*

No, of course not. That was silly. I followed her line of vision, ready to tell her she had it wrong. It was dark, and she was more than drunk, and clearly a fine, upstanding individual like Michael would never set foot in a club like this. But when my eyes reached the edge of the dance floor, which was incidentally, just when Dane took my earlobe into his mouth, I caught sight of him.

Michael. Arms crossed, still as a sentry among the writhing crowd, and staring at me, absolutely stone-faced.

TWENTY-SIX

So that *was* him.

Michael. Here, in a seedy club.

Though his face was stone, it wasn't unreadable. Michael's usual face was permanently pleased, with just about everything. He always looked as if he was delighted, even when things didn't go to plan. But his impassive expression told me, without a doubt, that I'd done something wrong.

Maybe it had to do with Dane's tongue in my ear?

The liquid courage pulsing through my veins said, *Well, that's fine and good. He lied to you, Frankie. He deserves it.*

If it had been Piers, looking at me that way, I'd have been proud of myself. So often he'd be disappointed in me for the silliest things, like my outfit, or picking up the wrong brand of milk at the store. But Michael? If he showed disappointment, it was for a good reason. And Michael's disapproval was more than sober or drunk Frankie could bear.

Feeling the heavy weight of guilt on my shoulders, I pried Dane's arms off me and slipped out of his embrace.

"What are you doing?" He asked me, trying to pull me back. I managed to shake him off as he looked up and caught sight of Michael. He grinned. "Oh. Things are about to get interesting, huh?"

No. I hoped not. Part of me might've been aching to teach Michael a lesson, but I still wasn't the type to want to do it with an audience nearby.

I put a hand on his chest. "Not in the least. Everything's fine."

"We're leaving, right?"

No. Seeing Michael there made it so confusing. I was still bitter, but his presence made the reality of what I was about to do come crashing down upon me. I'd be shagging Dane out of spite. Nothing else. And how would I feel in the morning? I wouldn't have Dane, nor would I really want him either. I sure as hell wouldn't have Michael. I wasn't certain what my aim was, anymore, but it definitely wasn't launching myself head-first into major depression, again.

I held up a finger and ordered Dane, like he was Saucy, "Just stay. Wait right here."

His lips twisted. I think he already knew I was about to leave, and never come back. He didn't fight it. And how's this for a perfect indication of how much I meant to him? Before I'd even turned my back to him, he was already humping the leg of another woman in a skimpy halter dress, as she showed off her moves on the dance floor.

The crowd seemed to part like the Red Sea as I made my way over to Michael. When we were toe-to-toe, I eyed him defiantly. "Why are you here?"

His stone face looked graver, now. Like he was ruing the loss of our relationship. "Frankie—"

"Oh, do stop looking like a lost puppy, already. This is on you. It's not my fault in the least. You lied to me!" I'd been raising my voice, and the last sentence coming during a break in the music. To my chagrin, a couple of people stopped grinding to the music and turned to look at us. It hurt my heart to be mean to Michael, but I was in the right and I had to be strong.

Embarrassed, I stalked away. The second I got to the main steps, I felt exhausted, from head to toe. This night was over.

Michael caught up with me as I was reaching the front door. He grabbed my wrist. I closed my eyes, too tired to even think about getting into this with him now; I couldn't admit it then, but I was ashamed of what I was planning to do tonight and what had already happened with Dane. I wanted to sleep on it. Compile my thoughts. Anything I said now would be nearly incoherent, due to my fatigue and tipsiness.

I slipped from his grip and pushed out the door. It must've been early because there was still a crowd of people, waiting to get in. I rushed past them, toward the street, hoping to flag down a passing cab. But there were none. Michael was hot on my heels, calling my name.

I tried to skirt away, but Michael clearly seemed intent on hashing this out now. "Stop," he said, with increasing frustration. "Stop."

At the edge of the curb, I searched desperately, up and

down the street. Not a taxi to be had. I unzipped my purse to pull out my phone so I could order one. Meanwhile, Michael was still there, my shadow, willing me to stop what I was doing and focus on him. "Frankie. Could you listen to me?"

I should've known. Michael was not one to toss in his hand and give up. I clucked my tongue and looked up at the dark sky, refusing to meet his eyes. "What?"

I expected another apology. I expected excuses. But when Michael opened his mouth, something entirely unexpected came out. "Haven't you been checking your phone?"

"No," I said, fishing it from the bottom of my purse, where it'd been since I arrived at the club. "Did you call me?"

"Yes."

I checked the display. Sure enough, I had a list of texts and voicemails.

"Well, what did you expect? For me to hang around, waiting for you to call and ex—"

"Frankie." His voice was firm. A warning.

Something was off.

I looked down at the display again. Yes, some of the calls were from Michael. But there were just as many from Jessica.

I opened a text from Jessica. It said, simply: *Call me when you get this.*

I groaned. What, were he and Jessica the best of friends, now? Before the last New Year's party, they hadn't said more than ten words to each other. The thought of them conspiring together about me, behind my back, made me feel ill.

I held it up to him, disgusted. "What is this? What the fuck do you two think you're doing? Making decisions about my life, without me? Again!"

He squinted to read it, a confused expression on his face. "Wait. Frankie, listen to—"

Out of the corner of my eye, I spied a flash of yellow. A cab pulled to the curb, right beside me, letting out a gaggle of women in clubbing clothes, marinating in a sweet-smelling cloud of heavy perfume and hair product.

"I've got to go," I mumbled to him.

"Frankie, could you listen to me for a moment?"

But I was done listening to people who professed to know more about my life than I did, who "wanted to help" but wound up mucking my life up more.

"Oh, fuck off, would you?"

One of the girls looked at me, then burst out laughing. I gave her the finger. The moment the last girl vacated the cab, I slipped in and slammed the door myself, feeling satisfied with myself. "Four Seasons."

The cab took off. I peered through the rear window at Michael, who had his hands in the pockets of his slacks and was watching me, that impassive expression on his face again. He was still staring after me as the cab turned a corner and sped out of sight. It gave me a hint of pleasure to know he'd likely be thinking about me, tonight, too. With Piers, I'd never thought as much; when I left Piers, for a minute or a week, I'd always had the feeling it was out of sight, out of mind.

I spent the next few moments, deleting all of Michael's messages without reading them, so I wouldn't be tempted to respond. Then I looked at Jessica's. *Call me when you get this.*

Jessica was a bit of a wizard, especially when it came to men. Just what I needed, to have to listen to her say, *I told you so* about Michael, when I was already feeling like such a shit. Or maybe he'd convinced her to put in a good word for him.

Not happening.

Fine. I'd call … but I wouldn't let her say anything. I'd tell her to stop conspiring and butt out of my life. I jabbed in her number.

"There you are! I've been going mad trying to get in touch with you!" she said at once. Her voice was foreign. She sounded frantic. "Michael has, too, but he said you wouldn't listen to him."

I slumped back against the seat. "So you know all the sordid details, I'm sure. Have you called to gloat? Speak on his behalf? Is that it?"

"I don't know what you're talking about. I'm sure it has something to do with Michael, but you can fill me in later. I've been trying to get in touch with you because your father is in the hospital. He had a heart attack at work, earlier today."

My heart thudded to a stop in my chest. I moved to the edge of the seat and reached for the door handle, wanting to escape. Wanting to be there, in London, now. But of course, I couldn't be. I was stuck.

"What?" I couldn't breathe. "Is he okay?"

"He's in the ICU, but they won't tell me anything because I'm not family. Michael and I have been trying to get in touch with Alex, but no go. He's not responding to texts. Frankie—" She paused. "Are you all right?"

No, I wasn't. I looked around helplessly. So all that time, Michael hadn't been trying to apologise. He'd been trying to delicately break the news. And I'd … told him to fuck off.

Oh, god.

"Fine. Just fine," I lied, my voice wooden. "I'll be on the next flight home."

TWENTY-SEVEN

Ten hours later in the late morning, the taxi pulled up at University College Hospital in London. I hadn't had time to breathe in the air, to revel in finally being back on home soil. I hadn't slept in over twenty-four hours. All I could do was think of my father, lying in a hospital bed. My poor father had been so strong, while my mother was alive. Now, it seemed all but inevitable that this would happen. His heart had been breaking, ever since she'd died.

And I'd gone and left him.

Because of Michael's bright idea. Michael had likely convinced my father it was a great plan to let me go a quarter of the way across the world to set my life straight, that it would help me. And look what it did. It left me stranded, where I couldn't be with my father when he needed me.

When the driver looked back at me, wondering why I hadn't paid the fare yet, I realised my hands were clenched into fists. It had taken a long plane trip, but now, I was starting to feel livid about Michael.

I quickly swiped my card and stepped out with my carry-on luggage. Then I rushed into the hospital. Five minutes later, I was in the ICU, at the door of my father's room, listening to the doctor bat about phrases like "mild myocardial infarction" and "non-invasive echocardiogram" and "increased risk for stroke." I nodded along, not fully processing any of it, even when I was informed that he was in good condition and stable. I just wanted to see him, then I'd know he'd be okay.

This looked anything but stable.

He looked so fragile and old as if he'd aged ten years in the time I'd been gone. His pock-marked scalp shone through his translucent greying hair under the fluorescent lighting, which amplified his sallow, grey-green complexion. Wires and tubes invaded his slight body, disappearing under his hospital gown. His mouth was slightly open in his sleep, but I couldn't help feeling like it was an expression of pain.

He'd said to me, right after my mum died, that he wanted to go along with her. Right now, he looked about ready to do just that, as if he'd given up.

Almost without realising it, I wound up at his bedside. I took his hand. It was surprisingly warm but even so heavy and lifeless, the texture not of skin but of waxed paper. "Dad?"

Nothing.

My eyes misted with tears. He couldn't leave me. Now, more than ever, I needed him. I didn't have anyone else who believed in me wholeheartedly.

I stood there, listening to the machines steadily whirring, envisioning my life without him, and at that moment, more than ever, I was sure I'd made a mistake.

I'd left him.

I'd left to escape a relationship gone bad. But I'd escaped the good things in my life, too. My friends. My home. What was left of my family. Maybe ... maybe things weren't that terrible before. I'd gone off to find greener pastures, and was I happy, now?

No. Not even close.

A tear slid down my cheek, and I wiped it away, just as a voice said, "Frankie?"

I looked up. Piers.

There he was, in the flesh, standing in the doorway. I hadn't seen him in four months. He'd grown out his hair and become paler. Put on a little weight, too, perhaps. But he still looked fine, in his custom-tailored suit, like someone you'd see in a crowded room and want desperately to look your way.

Though that was what had got me in trouble all those years ago, in a basement party at uni, something was different. The swagger was gone. He looked almost ... remorseful.

I refused to buy it. "Piers. What are you doing here?"

He pointed behind him. "I managed to convince the nurse that we were engaged," he said with an innocent, charming shrug. "It's not a lie. We *were* engaged."

I could see him, sweet-talking the ladies at the nurses' station, making them giggle as he effortlessly drew them to his side. The thought made me bristle. I rolled my eyes "And?"

"I heard about your old man. I wanted to see if there's anything I might do?"

I shook my head woodenly. "No." There wasn't anything I could do. It was too late to do anything to help him. He was now at the mercy of the medical staff.

A nurse arrived and beamed at Piers, but Piers ignored it, taking in my father's condition. She seemed disappointed as she went to my father's side and took his vitals. "I'm sorry, Ms Benowitz, but visiting hours are over."

I nodded. My father hadn't moved, probably didn't even know I was there. I supposed it would do me good to take a shower, get something to eat, grab some shut-eye, since I hadn't done any of those things in over twenty-four hours. "All right. I'll be back. What time can I—"

"You can come by any time after eight."

"All right. I'll be here at eight on the dot," I promised, turning to the door.

When I looked at Piers I realised I had no idea where to go. I supposed it made sense to go to my family home. Luckily, I still had a key on me.

"I have my car. Do let me drive you," he said, pulling out the keys to his Porsche.

I nodded, yawning. I didn't want to have to make any more decisions.

Ten minutes later, I was where I swore I'd never be again—in Piers' car, weaving through city traffic on the way toward Hampstead. Even as I sat there, feeling déjà vu, I told myself I would not entertain conversation with him. I'd pretend this was a taxi and that we were strangers.

But of course, Piers had other ideas. He was never one to be in a room with another person, silent, for long. It was why he drove me crazy whenever I wanted to spend a quiet evening reading. "Don't worry. Your father's a tough old bugger. He'll get through this."

I certainly hoped, but I'd promised myself I'd never believe anything Piers said again. "Hmm."

"I've heard you're doing well in the States."

I nodded and turned toward the window, watching the streetlights making crystals on the rain-spattered glass. I hoped that would tell him that conversation was off limits.

"Good for you, Frankie. That's brilliant." He paused for a beat, then let out a long sigh. It confused me because Piers was never one to look beaten. He always cleverly hid such things. "Things have not been so well for me."

I turned to look at him. The lines on his face made him look older, too. He'd definitely changed, become more fragile. He wanted me to talk, and that was the only topic that would pique my interest, where Piers was concerned. Looking back, I suppose he knew that. "They haven't?"

"No. I was sacked from my job a month ago. Got a new one, of course, but I can't say I'm that keen on it. Moved out of the place on the Heath, too. Something smaller. A bachelor pad."

He didn't say the obvious, which was that he couldn't afford it. Though Piers had made a good living, the truth was that we had needed my trust fund to help make our monthly payments. And knowing his penchant for engaging in expensive hobbies, fine dining, and the like, I wondered if that meant he was broke.

"That's a shame. I liked that house in Hampstead."

He nodded, staring straight ahead. When we pulled into the drive of my father's place and I looked up at the darkened windows, déjà vu again invaded. How many times while we were dating had he driven me home to a darkened house, long after my parents had gone to sleep? Sometimes, we'd fool around in the driveway, since we didn't have a place that was ours. Once, right here, I'd given him a blow job. I felt nervous and vulnerable at the memory like Piers could see what I was thinking.

I felt a pang of dread. This time, when I went inside, I'd be alone. I wouldn't hear my father snoring. My mother wouldn't come out of the room in her housecoat, bleary-eyed, asking me if I'd had a good time. The house would be cold, empty, and forlorn.

Piers seemed to sense my regret because he cut the engine before I could open the door.

He turned to me. "The thing is, Frankie love, nothing has been the same since you left me."

Before I knew what was happening, he'd taken my hand.

"I lost you," he said, stroking my palm with the pad of his thumb. "I lost my good luck charm."

I shook my head. This was wrong. "Piers, I've got to—"

"How do I win you back? Tell me. Because whatever it is, I'll—"

"No. You *can't*. It's over. You—"

He dropped my hand. "There has to be some way. Look, you can't walk away from your commitments. You're not a child. Don't you think you've punished me enough?"

I could see it in his eyes. For Piers, no never meant no. It meant that eventually, if he kept pushing and prodding the right buttons at the right time, he'd get there. But he was past the point of acting sad and desperate. He was inching his way into anger, into saying things to make me feel bad, so that I'd eventually crumble. That's what he did. He swooped in when a person was at their weakest and used it to his advantage.

And as I looked up at that empty house, I felt weak. Hopeless. I wanted more than anything to have a shoulder to lean on, right now. But the only one available to me was the one I swore I'd never touch again.

"I've got to go." I pushed open the door.

"I'll be here at seven. Tomorrow. To pick you up, all right?" he called, a softness edging back into his voice.

I would've argued, but I was simply too tired.

"All right," I mumbled, feeling like shit, even before I entered the empty house of my childhood, a house that I knew would never again feel as safe and warm as it once had, in those idyllic years while I was growing up.

TWENTY-EIGHT

The house was, as I expected, bleak.

As exhausted as I was, when I changed into pyjamas and climbed into my childhood bed, I couldn't sleep. Everything in my bedroom held a memory—the curtains with pom poms my mother had picked out because, she said, *Frankie, they're so YOU!* The legal textbooks my father had given me when I was twelve, because he'd thought that my wanting to be on the debate team meant that I'd follow in his footsteps and pursue law. The photograph of me and my parents on the day I graduated from uni. And the presents my father had brought back from the various countries he visited for work. A big cuddly panda sat on my bed that he'd brought back from China a few years ago. It served as my comforter after my mother had died.

Walking into any bar on campus on Piers' arm, I *meant* something. People immediately gravitated to us, the power couple. I'd had the job with *Slip,* then, too, and had already written my first piece for them. The editor had gushed that she could feel it—I was going to make my mark on the world.

I wanted the girl in that photograph back.

I climbed out of bed and picked up the frame, staring

at it. My parents were the same; only the girl in between them was different. She was someone I didn't know. She was excited, full of spark, ready to make that mark.

And now I was lost, sinking. It started with my mother's death. If I lost my father, would I only slip further?

The thought terrified me.

I needed him. Oh, I could do things for myself, but in the end, I needed an anchor. There was a time that I thought Piers was that anchor.

Now, I felt like I was drifting off to sea. No course, no idea where I'd eventually land.

As I was staring at the photo, my phone rang. It was Jessica. At that second, I realised I hadn't told her I'd arrived in town. I picked up and as I was bringing it to my ear, she said, "Were you ever going to tell me you landed?"

"Sorry, I—"

"You saw your father, didn't you?"

I sniffled, and it was at that moment, I realised I was crying.

Her tone suddenly turned soft. "Oh, honey."

"I'm sorry," I said, wiping my eyes. "I'm overtired. But he looked so sad there, so fragile. He was asleep. Jessica, he's always been there for me, and I wasn't here for him. I feel so … rotten."

"Rubbish, Frankie! You're a good daughter. The best! And your father is going to be fine." I could almost hear the gears turning in her head. "How about this? I'll pick you up bright and early, we'll grab some breakfast, and then we'll head over to the hospital."

It sounded lovely. I really needed her shoulder to cry on. But then I remembered. "I can't. Piers came to the hospital. He said he'd—"

"What does that wanker have to do with anything!" she shouted into the receiver. "Oh, my, God, Frankie! Don't tell me you're back with him?"

"No. Of course not."

"Well, that's what he's trying for, you know. He's weaselling his way in there. Did you hear he got sacked from his job? And he's been making the rounds at every pub in London. He's seriously gone off the rails, Frankie. And he is grabbing for a lifeline. Don't be his lifeline, he'll sink you to stay afloat."

"I'm not going to fall for that. Believe me," I said, even though it was silly. In this state, I didn't believe myself.

"So call him and tell him to fuck off."

I gnawed on my lip. "Why don't we meet for dinner, tomorrow instead?"

"Frankie—" Her tone was a warning.

But even though the rope was frayed, I didn't want to let go of the Piers lifeline. It felt like the only one I had left.

"Tomorrow? We can go to that Argentinian place you like on Heath Street."

"Frankie—"

"Say, eight?"

She didn't say anything, but she let out a sigh of acceptance. I quickly ended the call, assuming it was a date.

Then I ran my finger over the picture of my mother. She had such a kind face. I'd got my flawless skin from her, but she had dark, wayward hair that always seemed to be falling in her face. It smelled like vanilla shampoo. I inhaled, wishing I could smell that, but the house was musty as if it'd been closed up since her death. And it had been. All light, all good things, gone. Even my weekly casseroles for my dad hadn't helped. Maybe nothing would.

That photograph made me wonder where my mother had kept the others. Now I thought about it, in the weeks after her death, my father had gone through them all. I'd often catch him in the kitchen, picking through old shoe-boxes. There'd been dozens.

I jumped out of bed, then rushed to their bedroom. The bed was neatly made and though my mother's side hadn't been slept in for over a year, no-one would have known it. The case for her reading glasses was still on the bedside table, along with a dust-covered mystery novel. It was like it was waiting there, patiently, to be picked up again.

I found the photos in my mother's closet. Of course, they were all there, organised by date. My mother was a big fan of photographs. Everywhere we went, she'd tote around her compact Polaroid, and snap pictures of absolutely everything. And they were all here, documenting a life before. A life when things were happy.

Pulling out shoebox after shoebox, I piled them on my parents' bed and one by one pulled off the lid. Not wanting to disrupt my mother's careful cataloguing, I went through them methodically, with great precision, staring with the pictures from their honeymoon, when

I was merely a glimmer in their eyes. Then photographs of them with Alex, and with me, and every single school event I was ever part of.

Funny—since my mother was so photograph-happy, she'd been the one taking all the photos. But she was in very few.

As soon as I noticed that, I began tearing through them, looking for more. The one photograph I had, in my bedroom, was the best one. And yet, it didn't tell much of her. It was simply a 2D rendering of a person, flat and failing to show the thousands of other moods and faces a person can show in life. But even if I'd had a million photos of her, I knew it'd never do justice to the real person.

I found another picture of my mother, which was an overexposed shot of the top quadrant of her face, one that must've accidentally been taken when she'd gone to check the film or fix the flash. One dark brown eye, same as mine, stared at the camera, and that wayward dark hair of hers tumbled onto her forehead.

I hugged the photo to my chest, catching a sob in my throat, lay back upon the pillows, and stared at the ceiling. Somehow, I fell asleep.

TWENTY-NINE

Like a doting husband, Piers picked me up exactly on time.

I took my time walking out to the car, meanwhile going through all the things I'd thought about, last night.

Jessica was right. Piers was a wanker. There was no doubt about that. But maybe *was* was the operative word. No one is perfect. And contrary to the popular notion about leopards not changing their spots, *sometimes*, people did. Something big, life-changing, happened to them, and their whole lives flashed before their eyes. Maybe losing me had forced Piers to go through one of those Road to Damascus moments, and he was a changed man.

That thought cycled through my mind as I slid into the front seat of his soft top.

"What's the matter?" he said immediately, leaning in to kiss my cheek.

"What do you mean?"

"You have a queer look on your face."

"Oh. I was thinking about that pub we used to go to. You know. That hole in the wall near the university? We were such a *team* at that place. Like royalty. I doubt the place would even open without us there."

"Ah." He grinned. "The Red Lion. You used to dance on the bar."

I nodded and laughed. "Yes. I did. After one too many."

"You had the best legs of all the girls." His eyes drifted to them. I'd had a thing for wearing the shortest skirts, in those days. "Those videos we made—the ones in my dormitory? Pretty hot. You knew how to be wild."

I flashed to a few drunken moments, with his phone, snapping me on his bed. I'd been naked, spread out so I left nothing to imagination, trying to be seductive for him. At the time, I'd had an inkling it was a mistake, but I'd been Frankie the Invincible. Nothing could touch me. And Piers *worshipped* me, rightly. I thought we would be together forever. "Wait, what? You don't still have those, do you?"

He shook his head. "Of course not. That was years ago."

I let out a sigh of relief. "Good. That, I'm not sure I want to preserve for posterity."

"Yeah. I know." He grinned. "But I wouldn't have minded holding onto them."

Blushing, I quickly changed the subject. "You used to be the pool champion. Remember when you got into a fight with that guy? The one who was twice your size?"

"That was over you."

"Over me?"

"Yeah. He had a thing for your legs, too."

I wasn't sure that was true, but I supposed it didn't matter. "If it weren't for your mates ... I thought you were done for."

He laughed. "Oh, yes. I remember. I thought I was, too."

I found myself laughing harder as we reminisced, and it was almost like old times. As we drove to the hospital, I couldn't help it. I ached for that old me. I wanted it back. And maybe Piers was here, in my life, now, because of it.

When we pulled up to the hospital, he started to roll into the parking garage, but I shook my head. "Piers. Can you let me go in myself?"

He frowned. "Nonsense. I—"

"Please. I need some alone time. But I'll call you later, all right?"

He nodded. "Sure. Call me. I'll pick you up. We can have lunch?"

"Yeah. Sure." I forced a smile.

As I reached for the door, he grabbed my hand. "Wait. Frankie. Wait." I looked into his eyes as he paused, collecting his words. "I wanted to let you know … it's really good seeing you again. And being apart, I've thought a lot about us. And I hope you have, too."

"I have," I admitted.

"We belong together, Frankie. You know it. All signs point to us. Like you said. A team." He said with a sincerity that triggered an anxiety spike in my stomach.

He squeezed my hand in both of his, and for a moment, I thought he might try to kiss me. He didn't, thankfully. If I was working my way back to him, I didn't want to go full-speed. I had to be cautious, or Jessica, Alex, none of them would ever understand my reasoning. I needed to keep my wits about me.

Even though I was feeling a bit of hope about Piers finally seeing the error of his way, there was something dark and hollow in the bottom of my stomach. The unease seemed to grow as I took the elevator to ICU.

When I got to my father's room, something was different. His face seemed to have more of its colour. His eyes were closed, but he looked more like himself. I pulled a chair in close and sat down. "Hello, Dad."

I didn't expect an answer, so I was astonished when his blue eyes fluttered open. They wandered lazily about the room for a good ten seconds before landing on me. The open mouth stretched into a smile. He wheezed, "Frankie, darling. You're here."

My heart gave a leap.

"Of course I am. Of course." I wanted desperately to jump into his arms and hold him, but the wires, and his frail body, stopped me. "I came as soon as I heard. Can I get you anything?"

He shook his head slightly. "How is the job?"

I laughed. Always so focused on work, which was how he'd grown his firm into one of the best in London. "It's fine. But you need to rest."

"All I've been doing is resting." He shuffled in bed and seemed a bit more of his old self. I helped him fluff his pillows so he could sit more upright. "I'm glad you're here because I wanted to tell you ... I'm so proud of you."

"Oh," I said, my heart sinking. "You already told me."

"Not in person."

He'd been so happy the last time I'd called, when I told

him about my column in *Miami Scene.* I'd gushed like a teenager with her first crush, and he'd gone on and on about how proud he was that I was making my mark in the world, and how he knew I could do it. *My talented daughter, so brilliant!* he'd said. But that was before I knew the truth.

"Actually, about that—" I started with a shrug. "It's not the big deal I thought it was. I didn't realise that Michael got me the job. I thought you had."

"We didn't *get you* the job. We made inquiries. That's all."

"I didn't even have to interview."

"Because your experience spoke for itself."

"Right. Michael essentially threatened them that they needed to take me on as a columnist."

His eyes narrowed. "Frankie. Michael is an excellent litigator. But if you think he has even one threatening bone in his body, I'll tell you right now. You're wrong."

That was true. It wasn't in his nature. But it didn't make any sense. "But how else—"

"Maybe he just suggested, and they did the rest of it themselves. They read your work. They saw how brilliant you are. And you *are* brilliant. Your work is top-notch. If only you'd believe it."

I shook my head. "I'm not—"

"You *are*. But when you talk like that, you're not the smart, headstrong girl your mother raised. You know who you sound like? That damned ex of yours."

The harshness of my father's words struck me like a

slap across the face. My Dad may have been a lawyer, but he was a negotiator, not a bulldog. "But ... you *liked* Piers."

He laughed softly. "I liked him because *you* liked him. And I think it's important, for preservation of the family, to get along with my son-in-law, regardless of my personal opinion of him."

"So, you—"

"He was not the right man for you, Frankie. He put it in your head that you weren't good enough. I'd hoped you'd have worked him out of your system by now."

"I have! I've—" I froze. His words jarred me. I hadn't seen how deep everyone's disdain was for Piers. Hadn't wanted to. What the hell had I been thinking, outside, on the curb, mere moments before?

"Yes, you have. And I'm proud of you. You went all the way across the Atlantic and started over. Not many people have the guts to do that."

"Oh, I only did it because I had Daddy's money backing me up. Otherwise—"

I trailed off, realising I *was* guilty of what he was accusing me of.

He patted my hand lovingly. "But you haven't worked his voice out, yet. Eventually, I think you will."

He was right. Even while Piers was gone, I was letting his ghost dictate everything I should feel. I was even letting his ghost tell me I should run right back to him, after months of getting over him.

And ... fuck that. I was smarter than that.

The second it came to me, I knew it was right. "You're absolutely right, Dad."

"I know. I've been around the block a time or two," he said, stroking my hand. "But don't worry. I have a few good years left in me."

Tears sprang to my eyes. "You do?"

"Oh, yes. This is nothing. The doctors say I can go home in a few days. You haven't seen the last of me yet."

I smiled and kissed his fingertips. "Oh. I am so glad to hear that!"

"I know," he said, beaming at me, and I decided that look, the one he was giving me, was nothing Piers could ever give. It was one that showed he didn't just love me, but that he'd go to the ends of the earth for me.

And I knew what I had to do.

I grabbed my phone and texted Jessica: *Pick me up for lunch?*

THIRTY

True to her word, Jessica picked me up and whisked me off to our favourite café in Mayfair. Sitting in a window seat across from Hyde Park, I couldn't help but feel nostalgic for the days we used to enjoy long lunches from our careers, discussing everything from politics to inconsequential things, like where we were going on holiday and exes we'd bumped into.

Now, though, I felt like a different person. A thousand years older and wiser.

After Jessica asked how my father was, and we exchanged the usual pleasantries about our families and our health, the topic of conversation swerved quickly toward the train wreck that was my love life. After all, it'd always been a favourite of Jessica's, and the one thing she knew, without a doubt, that she would be able to offer sage advice on. Jessica always saw herself as a talk-show host, helping the lovelorn through their dating quandaries. She should've had her own column in a magazine.

"Yes, so it turns out," I started, knowing this was the question she had on her lips. "Piers *does* want to get back together with me."

"Wanker," she muttered under her breath. "Of course he does. And?"

"And … don't worry about it. I'm not falling for it. Not in the least. We're done."

She eyed me cautiously. "Are you sure?"

"Absolutely. It's funny. Part of the reason I always stayed with him is because I thought I couldn't do any better. Marry within high society, live that ivory-tower existence where we're admired by everyone as a shining example of the perfect couple. I thought that was what my parents *wanted* from me." I shook my head. "But can you believe it … my father never liked Piers? He admitted that to me."

She let out a snort. "Of course he didn't."

I stared at her. "What? You knew?"

"Well, no one really did. But we all thought he was totally wrong for you. The longer you were with him the more you had changed, and not for the better. I mean, we were trying to be nice, because you clearly loved him, and if you were happy, who were we to tell you to put the brakes on? But," She shuddered. "He was terrible for you. Everyone was happy when you called off the wedding."

The more I stared at her, the more I realised she was right. The signs were there, all along. People I was close to never seemed to want to visit any more, when it was me and Piers. As much as we'd closed ourselves off from others, they'd done the same … and why? Because Piers was insufferable. They'd put up with him, for me. But they didn't *like* him. "Oh."

The waiter came, and she quickly ordered us our usual—two chopped salads and house white. "What about Michael?" she asked once the waiter had left.

I sighed. "What about him?"

"That doesn't sound good."

"Well … it's over. You're right. He wanted to control me. He jockeyed me over to Miami for the job without even asking me, without taking into consideration my feelings. He engineered my promotion without my knowledge, making me look like a fool in front of my new colleagues and boss." I stared out the window miserably as a couple paraded by, holding hands and smiling at one another as if the rest of London didn't exist. "That's too much like Piers."

"Is it?" She wrinkled her nose.

I had expected her to agree with me. So her uncertainty was a surprise. "Isn't it?"

The waiter returned with our wine. She grabbed the glass by its stem and swirled it around like a sommelier, even though Jessica had never met a bottle of wine she wouldn't drink. "Not really. The way I see it, Piers wanted to fit you into the mould of the perfect wife, *for him*. Because it benefited *him*." She took a gulp and smacked her lips. "But what benefit did Michael get out of getting you that job? Nothing. He probably did it because he wanted you to be happy. He did it for you."

I stared at my wine; perhaps Jessica was right? By all accounts, when it came to love advice for other people, she was the Dalai Lama. As I sat there, I couldn't even remember why I'd been so angry at Michael in the first place. Because he'd helped me? Given me a step up to a job and a life I loved? "Oh, my God," I murmured. "You're right." It occurred to me that I hadn't even asked Michael what had happened with Gillian and I was taking Dane's word as gospel.

"So what are you going to do?"

I started rummaging around my purse for my phone. "I need to call Michael. He texted me, but I blocked his number." Why had I done that? That was so rude. I hadn't even done that to Piers.

"You're going to call him?" She seemed doubtful.

"Do you think I should go back to Miami? Talk to him in person?" I gnawed on my lip.

"You need to stop with the snap decisions, Frankie. Think for a moment. When's your flight back?"

"I just got a one-way ticket."

Her eyes widened. "You weren't going back?"

"No, of course I was." I'd left Saucy with Karla, and in my haste to leave I'd only taken my passport and a few small items that fit into a carry on bag. But truth be told, when I left Miami, I hadn't wanted to ever return. If I did, I expected it would just be for the things I'd left behind.

"What did Gillian say when you told them you had to come here?" she asked.

My mouth opened slightly. "Uh … oh. I might've forgotten to tell her I was going."

Jessica nearly choked on the gulp of wine in her mouth. She swallowed with some difficulty. "Darling. You can't do that."

"I know, but it was an emergency, and I was distraught, and—"

"But you've missed three days of work."

"Yes, but—"

We looked at each other and burst out laughing. What else was there to do?

Jessica was right, though. I wasn't myself with Piers, and I didn't know how to be myself after I'd left him. The old me felt like such a distant memory. I had been letting Piers live in my head rent-free since our split. Searching for the old Frankie was impossible—she was gone—and thinking about Piers every five minutes was muddying my decision making now. I needed to get off this hamster wheel.

I opened my phone. I didn't have any phone messages or texts from Gillian, so I assumed they were getting on, sorting projects and stapling just fine without me. Then I remembered I'd given human resources my Four Seasons room number as my contact. I'd intended to buy an American phone while I was living out there and update my details later, but never got round to it. So even if Gillian had wanted to get in touch with me, she wouldn't have been able to.

Quickly, I pulled up my work email box and found no fewer than sixteen emails, all from Gillian. I opened the first one, the subject of which was simply the date.

It's after 10 am, and you're not in the office. I've tried calling you unsuccessfully—hope everything's all right. Since you don't have any vacation or sick days accrued, I'm going to mark this down as an unpaid absence. Please see me when you do get in so we can discuss our absence policy.—G.

That sounded polite for Gillian. I was sure, once I told her about my father, she'd understand. Maybe, since then, Michael had told her.

But then I clicked on the last message, which was titled: *FYI.*

As of today, your employment at Miami Scene magazine has been terminated. Your personal effects have been collected and will be available for you to pick up at the main lobby reception area. Thank you.

"Oh, my gosh," I said, my skin buzzing with humiliation. "I've been sacked."

"You have?"

I set my phone down. "It's just a misunderstanding because I was MIA. I'll call her after this and settle things. I'm sure it'll be fine when I tell her why I was gone."

Jessica didn't seem to share my certainty. "I guess. You do have a valid excuse. But you made her sound inflexible."

"Oh, she is, but—" I nodded firmly. "I'll handle it."

She checked her watch. "Well, it's just nine in Miami. Maybe you should call her now?"

"You're right. I shouldn't make her wait any longer." I swiped my phone off the tablecloth and pushed my chair away. "Be right back."

As I walked toward the lobby of the building, I jabbed in the main number for the office. I spoke to a receptionist, who had me connected with Gillian's number. When she answered, it was with a terse, no-nonsense, "Gillian here."

"Hello, Gillian! It's Frankie Benowitz, here!" I said brightly.

There was dead air. A long, drawn-out period of it. That wasn't good.

"I'm sorry I disappeared on you. I was a bit distraught, you see. My father had some health issues, and I had to fly out to London right away to be with him. And in my grief and confusion, I must've—"

"That's no excuse." The words were flat. Final.

Actually, it was an excuse. A good one. Or, in my head, it was. "I'm sorry. I know I should've messaged you earlier. But now my father is on the mend, I should be able to come back out there in the next couple of days and—"

"Don't bother. You've already been terminated."

I swallowed. "Yes, well, I did get the message, but my father—"

"Frankie. You haven't been with us for very long. That type of behaviour doesn't fly. We need someone dependable. And we've already gone ahead and filled the position. So—"

"You have?" My heart dropped. It's been—what—twelve hours since she'd sent the termination message? How did they fill the job that fast?

"We had to. It was an important job that needed to be done. It couldn't stay open."

Right. The clicking-and-sorting simply couldn't wait. Truthfully, that part of my job, I didn't mind losing at all. As far as I was concerned, good riddance. "But what about my articles? And—"

"Feel free to send us things, freelance. We'll look them over and let you know."

"OK, I understand."

"Sorry, Frankie. I'd hoped this would work out."

I had, too. I only realised how much right then. This wasn't over, but I had more important things to deal with right now. *One disaster at a time*, I thought.

When the call ended, I held the phone to my ear, staring into space, annoyed at myself. I'd been on such a lovely upward trajectory, with or without Michael's boost, and now, I didn't have a job. I suddenly felt like I'd lost a limb, one of those *you don't know what you've got 'til it's gone* things. The crappy job ... Michael ...

I'd had it so good. And I'd fucked it up because I hadn't realised how much I cared about all of it.

Feeling as if someone had smacked me across the face, I wandered back to our table. Our salads had arrived, but I'd lost my appetite.

"So," I said when I sat down. "It appears I don't have a job any longer."

Jessica gave me a pout. "I was wondering. I'm sorry, sweetie." She reached a hand out to grab mine, and gave it a squeeze.

"Well, I suppose I only have myself to blame. I've had three days to send a quick email, and I cocked that up. I could've done it on the plane and been done with it."

"Are they still going to publish your articles?"

I nodded. "And she told me I can submit other stories, and they'd look them over. Freelance."

"Well, that's something! They know you're talented. And see? That has nothing to do with Michael. If he had been tying their hands behind their backs like you said, they wouldn't have sacked you. Right?"

"Right," I said lamely, though it did little to cheer me up. In fact, I felt like such a fool. I'd been acting like a silly schoolgirl since the New Year. I'd told Michael to go to hell, and all he was doing was putting in a good word for me to make me happy. God, could I possibly be any more daft?

My phone dinged with a text. I hoped it was Michael, but my excitement faded when I saw Piers' name. *Pick you up at the hospital? Argentinian place for dinner?* I paused over the message for a few seconds until Jessica's voice interrupted my thoughts.

"So what are you going to do?"

I answered, not taking my eyes off the message. "I think first, I'm going to start by meeting with Piers and telling him it's over. Then I guess I have to find Michael and tell him … I don't know what. I suppose *I'm sorry* is a good start."

She nodded and squeezed my hand again. "Yes, it is. You know what you want, Frankie. It's time you go and claim it."

Mind made up, I wanted to take the bull by the horns, right then. I almost told Jessica I wanted to cut our lunch short. But then she leaned in and said, "I hate bringing it up, because you have so much going on in your life. But I have news. Big news."

I eyed her carefully. Her big news was probably a new contract, or something fabulous that would have little to do with me, but would of course be worthy of my congratulations. But why did she look so leery? "Yes—" I prompted, as she looked over my head at someone- I thought the waiter, who she was going to order another drink from.

"I've kinda been seeing someone since New Year."

She was pink. In love. Why hadn't I seen this before? Jessica rarely got excited about men, but this one, whoever he was, had turned her into a blushing teenager. Agog, I said the words I never thought I'd utter to Jessica: "It's serious?"

She nodded and looked up at the person behind me. I realised it wasn't a waiter when he swept in and kissed my cheek. Practically jumping out of my chair, I snapped my neck to the side and took in the man beside me.

It was Alex.

• • •

For a good fifteen minutes, I watched my best friend and brother fawning over one another, clearly besotted with each other, my mouth slightly open.

Alex was finally not behaving as if he was the only person in his universe. He noticed her drink was empty and asked the waiter to refill it. He held her hand. Gazed at her like she was the most amazing thing he'd ever seen. They were cute. A handsome couple.

How had I never seen this before?

I sat there, watching this, unable to eat my meal as Jessica told me of how they had fallen into each other's arms that night, and couldn't help themselves after that. With all the other stresses in my life swirling around me, I didn't know what to say. Disgust bubbled up. They'd been seeing each other since New Year? And never said a word, even though I'd called her about a hundred times since then? With everything going on, how could they think to unleash this bombshell on me?

And Alex—wasn't he the one trying to keep me from Michael? And here he was, dating my best friend? The betrayal was almost too much to bear.

I was about to throw my napkin down when Jessica stood up. She blew a kiss to me and said, "I am going to leave you two to it. I know there is a lot to catch up on."

I glared at him across the table. "I am sure we do."

He met my eyes for a moment before looking away. Oh, he knew he was in so much trouble. But then, he gazed adoringly up at Jessica as she squeezed his shoulder and came in for a kiss on the lips. It was sweet, intimate, and made me more than a little jealous.

And why not? My two favourite people, whom I loved dearly. What was not to love?

When she was gone, he said, "I just came from the hospital. Dad's ... wow. How did you find him?"

"Same as you." I glared at him, wondering if he was

going to ignore the elephant in the room forever. Then I sighed. Apparently so. "Don't be a muppet, Alex. Where have you been? Other than in bed with my best friend?"

He ran a finger over the rim of his wine glass. "Frankie. I meant to tell you. But … things progressed and we didn't want to jinx anything. I knew if people found out about us they would have a lot of opinions and I wanted to give it a fair shot. You know, before other people could get involved. Now we're … pretty close."

I snorted. "You've never been close with a woman."

"Yeah. I know. But Jessica … she's different."

I knew that. Did he think he could tell me anything I didn't already know about my best friend? I opened my mouth to tell him, but it suddenly hit me. Jessica was the female Alex. She worked hard, played harder … dated and slept around but never found anyone that she imagined keeping around for longer than a few nights. For the two of them to have stuck for all these months was … incredible.

"You're serious. You're not going to hurt her?"

He frowned, clearly offended. Then he said, "I know. I know I've been a shit to you, trying to keep Michael away from you."

"Yeah. Why have you been doing that, by the way?" I crossed my arms.

He shrugged. "I don't know. I hated seeing you with anyone. You're my little sister. I didn't think anyone was good enough for you. He was the first guy who tried to get to you, and so I told him you were off limits. On more than one occasion. But by the time I realised I couldn't do that when you were at uni and I was off on my own, you came back with Piers."

I glowered at him.

"The thing was. Piers couldn't give a shit what I had to say. Michael? He listened. Out of respect for the family. Which means he's probably a hell of a better guy for you than that wanker Piers ever was. I am truly sorry."

I still glared at him. "You're not saying this because you want my blessing to get in Jessica's pants, are you?"

He smirked. "I don't need your blessing for that. And don't be mad at her. She hated keeping this from you. But like I said, we both had to work out whether this was worth it before any outside influence ruined it."

I paused for a moment. The thought of the two of them, together like that, made me physically ill. But still ... the more I thought about it, the more it made sense. I never thought Jessica would find a happily ever after. I thought she'd be searching forever and never find the man who met her strict requirements. But she'd found Alex. And Alex, the perpetual playboy, had found her. They matched, it made sense.

"Okay, but you still haven't told me where you've been the past few days?"

"I went deep sea fishing with a few friends near the Azores. We knew our phones wouldn't work out there so we left them back at the hotel and took the satellite phone and radio. Jessica had been trying to reach me on the island for days." He paused for a moment and looked pensive, "I didn't think. I am so sorry. I have been so selfish since

Mum. Running off around the world, leaving you and Dad to pick up the pieces. I am gonna work on that"

He looked sheepish as he spoke, which was an unfamiliar sight. I put my hand on top of his and gave it a squeeze. Perhaps the thought of losing both parents had shaken him up?

His eyebrows tented, I could see how sorry he was. Resolving that there was no need to make him feel any worse I decided to change the subject.

"Wow, you're giving Jess your hotel details. You must really like her. So, does that mean Jessica and I ... might be sisters one day?"

I expected him to deny it right out, since the M-word was a dirty word, in his vocabulary. But he shrugged and said, "It's been discussed."

My eyes widened, before filling with tears.

Alex leaned forward and put a hand on mine. "Oh, sis. Don't cry. Shit, I didn't mean to make you cry. Is it really so terrible that we're together?"

I shook my head. "No," I said, my heart bursting with love for them both. "No. It's because it's so perfect. And because I love you two so much. I want to see you guys happy. I only wish that I can be that happy one day, too."

We got up and rushed around the table to hug tightly, so tightly I couldn't breathe. And I didn't mind, one bit. I felt like I had my brother back, for the first time since we were kids. Turns out, putting distance between two people isn't always for the best.

THIRTY-ONE

A few days later my father was being discharged from the hospital late in the evening, so I arranged to meet Piers at *La Cantina*, a couple of hours earlier. I was solving my problems one step at a time and it was Piers' turn next. As I took a taxi to the restaurant, I exchanged texts with Tori: *I am so sorry you lost your job! But you were MIA. We were worried about you.*

I wrote back: *It's all right. I might freelance. And I'll be coming back so we can have taco Tuesday again, soon.*

I didn't know if any of that was true, but it sounded good. I liked Tori and I could never thank her enough for taking me under her wing when I started at *Miami Scene*. I was learning how important it was to give your time to the right people, and Tori was one of those people.

I looked up and saw Piers, lounging at a window table and flirting with a short-skirted waitress, as I stepped out of the Black Cab. He turned and saw me, waving confidently as he sipped his scotch.

He'd already ordered an appetiser, their plantains in maple sauce. I *hated* plantains. It didn't matter that I'd told him that; he was under the impression they were good for me because they were fruit. The sickly sweet smell of them made my stomach roil as I sat down across from him. "Ordered you a rosé," he told me as he stood, took my hands, and kissed my cheek.

"I've learned rosés give me headaches," I explained, sitting down across from him.

"Everything gives you a headache," he mumbled with a snort, not looking up from his menu. But he snapped his fingers, anyway. The waiter obsequiously arrived by our table, a split second later. "Forget the rosé. Get her a—"

"Sparkling water," I said quickly. This time, Piers' eyes shot up in surprise. "Twist of lime."

No alcohol. I needed to be clear for what I was about to do.

When the waiter left, Piers dug into the appetiser letting the stringy syrup leave a trail between the serving dish and his plate. He scooped some into his mouth, then motioned for me to do the same. I could barely watch him chew. Oh, my god. He revolted me. It suddenly seemed so obvious to me, how wrong for each other we were.

I straightened in my chair. I needed to get this done quickly, like pulling off a wax strip. It didn't make sense to marinate in Pier's company for any longer than I absolutely had to.

"Look, Piers," I said quickly. "I'm not staying."

"You're going back to Miami?" He had syrup on his lips. "For how long?"

"No. I don't mean … I'm not staying here. At dinner. With you." I took a deep breath. "What I mean is that it's over, Piers. We're done. Unequivocally. Absolutely. "

He stared at me for a long time, chewing more slowly now. "You don't mean—"

"I *do*." My voice was firm and calm. Something he hadn't heard from me in a long time. I was done with him telling me what I meant to do. I definitely meant this, with every fibre of my being. I might not have had a job in Miami anymore, but it didn't matter. I needed to cut out the rot. And he was number one. "I'm sure of it. Don't think you can change my mind."

He swallowed, then stroked his jaw pensively, as if he was trying to compute this impossible information. Then, he blinked, as if he'd been gut-punched, and nodded. "All right. Wow. Okay. If that's the way you want to play it."

"I'm not playing anything, Piers. I'm ending things properly. We *can* be grown-ups."

He reached into his pocket of his slacks and pulled out his phone. I thought he was checking a text, probably from one of his girls, so I took the napkin off my lap and threw it on the table, pushing away.

I was about to tell him I'd see him around, wish him all the best, when he said, "Before you go—"

He set the phone on the table and turned the volume all the way up. It was playing a video. It looked like a lewd one. There were naked limbs, lots of skin. At first, I thought it was some cheap tacky porn, and wondered why on earth he'd be showing that to me, in a public place. But then I realised it was his private video. And the person on it, touching herself, was ... me?

I stared at it. I remembered doing it, years ago. I was so much younger then, had a swath of blue in my hair—that was popular at the time. In those early days I'd played myself off as more free-spirited than I actually was because I knew Piers preferred women who stood out. That made other men take notice. I'd made myself into that person, for him.

Which was why I'd let him take those videos of us, having sex. He'd loved them, at the time. Said I was the hottest woman on earth. And it excited me, thinking he'd use them for his pleasure when we couldn't be together. I thought he'd tucked them away, for his own enjoyment, and then deleted them.

But now I realise how trusting and naive that was. This was only the start of me, moulding myself to be Piers' ideal woman. He'd used my willingness to change for him to his advantage, all this time. Now he was still using me.

And from the look in his eyes, I knew he planned to use the videos, too. And not in the spirit of which they had been made.

I sat back down in my chair with a thud. "What are you … what are you doing?"

"I was thinking how your dad would react if he saw this," he said with a smirk. "I mean, his ticker's pretty terrible as it is. Knowing his daughter makes porn probably wouldn't help."

My jaw dropped. "You wouldn't."

"No, Frankie, that's where you're wrong. I would," he said with a sigh, pocketing the phone. "The thing is, you and I belong together. You might not be able to see it now, but you will. And I'm not above using certain tactics to get you to understand that. If I have to do it this way, I will. It's for your own good. This is why I am one of the most successful young bankers in London. I make the right decisions. I do whatever it takes to win. You should be my wife, Frankie. You will end up a nobody, on the shelf, without me. And in time you'll see this too. You'll probably thank me for this one day."

It's for your own good. How many times had he said that to me? And I allowed myself to be swayed by his bullshit? But Jessica was right. This was for *his* good. His family didn't have the kind of money mine did and he wasn't earning the kind of money I had, not yet. The truth was he needed *me*. He needed a wife who would always be there, be the *right* kind of wife and mother. That was all. And he knew I was the girl he could lead along on a chain if he broke me in the right way.

"You fucking bastard. How are *you* good for me?" I spat, my voice low. "You've never done a single thing for me. It's all about you, and what you want."

He circled his finger on the rim of his empty tumbler glass and leaned in. "Actually, *you* want me. Doesn't matter what I do. You've *never* been able to resist."

It was true. As much as I hated to admit it, he had a hold on me that I'd never gained control of. But now ... he disgusted me. And yet, I couldn't imagine what I'd do if my father saw that video. My friends. Everyone. What would everyone think? This video could haunt me forever.

I could never make a career for myself with this around my neck. The breakup with Piers was embarrassing enough. If I had to go through this? I might as well never show my face among London society, or my family, again. And not only that, *my father's* reputation would be in tatters.

I simply couldn't do that to him.

As much as I hated Piers at that moment, I couldn't. I couldn't be the person he was and only think of myself.

So I said, "My father's being discharged from the hospital soon. I have to go. Can you give me tonight to think about it?"

He nodded. Pulled out his phone and tapped away for a few seconds. My phone dinged. "A little something to remind you of what you're trying to keep out of the public eye," he said, smiling almost triumphantly. "You go to your father's, just for tonight. But ... darling. Don't take too long. There's no point in dragging this out."

THIRTY-TWO

"That's it, Dad. Nice and easy," I said, fluffing my father's pillows.

He climbed into bed and sighed as I pulled the covers up over his chest. "Enough with this rubbish, Frankie. I'm fine. Let's go downstairs and have some tea, shall we?"

"No, no, no," I insisted, pushing the covers back up when he tried to slip them off. "Your doctor said rest, and that means you need to rest."

"You sound like your mum," he groused.

I took it as a compliment. My mother always babied him. He needed babying. The lack of it was probably why he'd had the heart attack in the first place.

I planted a mystery novel I'd bought at the gift shop in his hands. "Read this. And do tell me if you need anything! I'll get it for you. Tea?"

He reached for his reading glasses on the bedside, but I sprang into action and grabbed them for him, opening them and plopping them on his nose. "No tea. Unless it will stop you hovering over me."

I pointed to the book. "Read it. It has good reviews. Let me know when you're sleepy and I'll come in and turn the lights out."

He peered over the rims of his glasses. "Oh, what's this rubbish you're giving me now? And now I can't turn the lights out myself?"

"It could be too much strain on your heart," I explained.

"Frankie. For the last time. The doctor said I'm fine. He said I could go back to the office next week! I just have to stick to the diet and take it easy."

"Which you *won't*," I warned. "You never take things easy. And you shouldn't be going to work."

He lifted the book and gave it a wiggle. "I'm going to read," he said with a tired smile.

"Good."

The moment I walked down the hall to my childhood bedroom, the smile I'd been forcing slipped from my lips. My father might have said he was fine, but I knew better. He was so fragile, now, a shadow of the man he'd been before mum died.

Just as I was starting to take control of my life, Piers pulled me back. Funny, months ago I'd been so desperate to be with him again, but now, all I wanted to do was get away.

And I couldn't. I'd have to build a life with Piers. Somehow. Could a life built on a lie survive? I cast my thoughts back to before, when I'd learned he was cheating on me it seemed like an eon had passed since then. I'd thought I could live with it, bury it. After all, there were plenty of society families that had their secrets and arrangements. I could be one of them, with my secret sex tape squirrelled away in Piers' safe-deposit box, as Piers went out and slept with whomever he wanted while spending my family's money. And what else could he blackmail me into? Where could this lead?

Better the money than my father. That video would destroy him, it'd destroy me. I couldn't let that happen.

Resigned to my fate, I changed into my pyjamas, brushed my teeth, and gathered my hair into a ponytail to wash my face. As I was scrubbing my face, thinking about the impossibility of the situation, the doorbell rang.

At first, I decided to ignore it. After all, it was after nine in the evening. But when the doorbell rang again, most insistently, I went to the foot of the stairs and crouched down to look out the sidelight. I could see someone standing there, wearing a suit, but couldn't make them out. My heart sank. I suspected Piers couldn't bear to afford me a last night of freedom, a last night with my father. Sighing, I went down and pulled open the door to find Michael.

"Michael!" I cried, so relieved and happy to see him that it came out as a breathless squeal. "What are you doing here?"

His suit was rumpled, he was carrying a leather roll-up garment bag, and he had that tell-tale five o'clock shadow—he'd just come from the airport. "I stopped at the hospital to see your father but must've just missed him. They said he was discharged tonight?"

I nodded, resisting the urge to throw my arms around him in a desperate embrace. "He's upstairs."

"Oh, if he's sleeping, then—"

"No. No, he's awake. And I'm sure he'd love to see you. He's getting fed up with my fussing, I think he's feeling like Paul Sheldon in *Misery.*"

I knew this, of course, because my father loved Michael. There wasn't a single time he'd have shooed him away. I stepped aside. "Come in, come in."

He did and dropped the heavy roll on the ground. "How is he?"

"Good. He should take it easy, but the doctor said he can go back to work next week."

He nodded, his eyes taking me in. "And how are you?"

I pulled self-consciously on some hair that had escaped my messy ponytail. "I'm good." I pointed up the stairs. "Right up there."

He started to climb the stairs but stopped. "Frankie—"

Inhaling sharply, I held up a hand. Seeing him there, knowing what could have been, and guessing at what he was about to say. It was too hard. Now, it felt like it was too late. "Don't. Michael, please. I enjoyed our time together, but the truth of the matter is, I've decided to go back to Piers."

"What?" He raised an eyebrow. "No, you didn't."

"*Yes*, I did," I argued, looking away. How disconcerting was it that I felt like he could see inside my brain, that he knew me better than I even knew myself. "So, I guess that's that."

He crossed his arms. "I don't think—"

"Dad!" I shouted, stepping away. "You have a visitor! Stay there! He's coming up!"

Michael gave me a look that said, *Did you have to do that?*

I shrugged. Yes, I did. Because I knew if I kept standing there, eventually, I'd crumble and tell him everything. He knew it, too, because he fixed me with a, *Don't go anywhere,* look before he started up the staircase.

Which meant I *had* to get out of there.

The second he stepped into my father's room and I heard the sound of their cordial conversation, I grabbed my coat from the hook and threw it on. Scuffing into my ballet flats, I quietly slipped out of the house and hurried down the street.

I walked through the darkened streets of my old neighbourhood, to the little place in Hampstead that Piers and I had almost called our family home. I stared up at it, wondering if that was going to be my life, making phenomenal pot roasts for the rest of my life, for a man I detested. Would I be able to be his wife, to have his children, to pretend we were a happy family? Could I live a life of misery and disdain for my partner?

I thought about my father. I thought about the video. I thought about Miami and Michael and everything in between.

Eventually, I wandered out to the Heath, and sat on the same bench I'd sat on months ago, after catching Piers in bed with that woman. The beginning of the unravelling.

I huddled in my coat, pyjamas and ponytail, staring into a black void until my toes were nearly frozen by the night chill. I was jolted back to reality by the sound of someone approaching rapidly behind me. I let out a high-pitched yelp, but then the figure plopped down beside me. "Cold out here."

"Michael," I said, giving him a sidelong glance. "How'd you know to find me here?"

"I didn't. I used to come here now and then when I lived in London. After noticing you were no longer at home, I felt like a walk. Truth be told I was hoping I'd find you avoiding me here"

I let his words sink in. "You came here ... before?"

"To see you. Yeah," he admitted, staring straight ahead of him onto the large grass common. "Not that I ever did, much. I wouldn't call it stalking. It's like my feet would sometimes find their way here. Like I said, not often, once or twice a year, maybe. But whenever I did, you were with him. So you didn't see me."

"Oh—"

"Piers changed you, you know."

I almost laughed aloud. "And how would you know that?"

"Are you kidding me?" He said sincerely, then continued "Whenever your dad would talk about you, at work, I'd always listen. He talked about you a lot while you were in uni, getting that job at the magazine, and on and on. His pride and joy. He loves you so much ... I guess I have been in love with you for a long time, too."

"Oh, but he was my father! Of course he'd say those thing—"

"But they're true. From the very first second I saw you, when we were kids, I knew it. Your smile was the best thing I'd ever seen. And so whenever your father would send me on a trip, I'd bring things home for you. Things I thought you'd like, things to make you smile. I'd give them to your dad, and tell him to give them to you."

I stared at him in surprise. Somehow, I didn't doubt it. Not knowing everything I knew about Michael. How he'd constantly been behind me, championing me. And I'd been so blind. But it'd always been him, lifting me up in small ways. The job in Miami wasn't the first time—it was just the time he'd been caught. "Those were from you? But why didn't you—"

"I told him not to tell you," he said, shaking his head. "I wanted to, but there was Alex, and I wasn't sure your father would approve. And then Piers came, and damned if he didn't steal that smile right from your face."

"But why would you—"

"You know why, Frankie," he said, turning to look at me. "Because it's always been you."

I swallowed hard, and tears sprang to my eyes, blurring everything. "Oh, Michael." I covered my face in my hands. "It's too late."

"No." He slid closer to me, pulling me to his warm body. I felt his breath fan against my cheek as he said. "It's not too late."

"It is. You don't know what Piers is like. You don't understand the lengths he'll go to so he gets what he wants. I can't be with you, Michael, not because I don't want to but because I can't. You see, Piers has something over me and he won't let me go … he … he has this—"

"Sex tape?"

I pulled my hands away from my face and stared at him, wide-eyed. "How on earth did you—"

"He's done it before, Frankie. A girl I went to uni with. Apparently, he makes women who trust him take those videos and send them to him. And then he blackmails them. Yes, *the* Piers Worthington's a real gentleman."

I stared in shock. "How do you know this?"

"I'm a lawyer, Frankie. She confided in me. Asked me to look into what could be done, while I was training. In the end, he'd lost interest in her and so she decided to let it be. And that was that. And imagine my shock when I realised that her ex-boyfriend was Piers Worthington, and he was your boyfriend."

My mouth opened, but words didn't come out for a full ten seconds. I nudged him. "Why wouldn't you tell me?"

"Would you have wanted to hear it? Besides, it would have totally wrecked your life. You seemed … happy. As long as you were, I didn't see it as my place to interfere."

"I wish you would've!" I said, hugging myself. "But I think you're right. Back then I wouldn't have wanted to hear it, and if you'd made me listen I would have called you and everyone else a liar." To think, this wasn't the first time Piers had done something so low. I already knew he was a cheater and a control freak. But I didn't see this kind of evil in him.

There was a silence between us for a few moments

before I spoke again. "I treated you so badly in Miami. I am so, so sorry. I know you, and I listened to gossip because I was so defensive about, well, everything. I felt I didn't know how to defend myself from all the other Piers Worthingtons of the world. Can you ever forgive me?"

"With everything Piers did to you, I'd be surprised if there weren't a few hiccups along the way." With that, he pulled me into an even tighter hug.

"So what can I do about Piers? I can't let this get out."

"Why don't you leave it to me?"

I blinked. He made it seem so easy. "What are you going to do?"

"Don't you worry. I think once he learns I'm onto him and that revenge porn carries a two-year jail sentence, he might think about backing down. Don't you?"

I nodded slowly. Yes, that would definitely get Piers to back off, but as I thought about it, I realised it wasn't what was upsetting me the most. I swallowed. "Don't you think badly of me? Knowing that something like that is out there? That I was so stupid?"

He laughed. "Oh, Frankie. You really think that? You matter to so many people. If that changes their opinion of you, I'd question whether *they* should matter to you, instead."

I nodded. He was right. Absolutely. "I imagine Piers would be mortified if a sex tape involving him got out."

"Yes. I suppose so. Which makes me think he's bluffing. He's all about appearances, that one."

"Absolutely."

"Feel better?"

I nodded again, a little absently, because something was coming to my mind.

"Good. Now, I left your father because I promised I'd run and fetch you, and he's also out of milk. So, shall we head back before we freeze our toes off?"

He stood up and offered me his elbow, which I jumped up and took. But before we could take a step back to the house, I hesitated. "Michael?"

"Hmm?"

"Thank you. For everything. For all you've ever done, for me and my family. I know it isn't enough, but—" I stood on my tiptoes and kissed the rough stubble on his cheek. "What if I took it from here?"

He tilted his head and looked at me. "That look in your eyes is nefarious. I love it."

I let out an evil laugh. As nervous as I was, I couldn't wait to get back to the house and set my plan in motion.

• • •

Late that night, when my father was long asleep, I went to my computer. With Michael sitting on my bed, encouraging me, I sent the video to my entire email contact list, with a note that said:

Dear friends,

Some of you may have been wondering why Piers and I broke up. Well, it turns out he was a very controlling person and cheated on me several times.

Recently, he has been making attempts to reconcile. Of course I refused. He's now trying to blackmail me into rekindling our relationship. His tool for this blackmail is a sex tape we made together. I don't want to allow him to control me anymore. Therefore, I'm taking my power back.

Here is our video. Look at it, or toss it away. I hope you'll understand.

Love,

Frankie

I looked back at him. He was lying on his back, comfortable on my bed. "It's done?" he asked.

I nodded.

"And how do you feel?"

"Good. Powerful." I smiled. "It's late. You should stay."

He sat up and looked around. "Here? Or—"

"Here's good." I put a knee on the side of the bed and slid to sitting. I put a finger to his lips to stop any protests. "Stop. My dad's asleep. And I love you. I love everything about you."

He tried to sit up more, but I placed a hand on his chest. I leaned over and put my mouth where my finger was, kissing his lips softly. He exhaled. "But your dad—"

I kissed him again, this time, deeper. He kissed me back, his hand tangling in my hair. I breathed in that heady sweet smell, not of any cologne, it was that uniquely Michael scent no one could ever bottle.

The moonlight spilled in from an open window. I

looked down at him then pulled my pyjamas off and cast them to the side. I undressed Michael and soon we were both lying in each other's arms.

He started to rock his hips against me and I felt him growing. Pulling me tighter into a bear hug. We stayed interlocked for a long moment until the desire to be as one was too much to deny ourselves.

"This is heaven," I whispered, savouring the feeling of his skin against mine. "I love this. I love being like this with you."

He buried himself in me completely. His forehead fell against mine as he moved, and he kind of crumpled there, motionless for a while. "Oh, Frankie."

He lowered his mouth against mine and kissed me. My hand trailed down the smooth curve of his back, and I felt a tremor between us. I couldn't be sure where it started and ended, because suddenly, we were one.

"I'm ... God," he breathed. "You were made for me, you know that? I don't want to move ever again."

"Then don't."

I don't know how long we stayed there, eyes locked, hips flush, hearts beating together. This moment was frozen in eternity, one I'd never forget, all my remaining days. He slowly pulled out, and I felt the slick, frictionless slide of him leaving me, coming out halfway, an emptiness that can only be filled by one thing. My hand gently nudged him back inside, and he got my hint, thrust into me, forcing the air out of my chest. I moaned.

His desire choruses with mine, a sound that made me

want more of him. His next thrust made me clench in pleasure, and the next time, I rocked in rhythm with him, meeting each thrust with my own.

Suddenly, he stopped, leaned over and steadied the headboard, his brow wrinkled in concentration. "Your dad."

I looked up at him, confused. I'd become so lost in him, again, I'd completely forgotten. I took his hand and drew it to my chest, urging him to keep going.

When we finished, as quietly as we could, he fell beside me. "I love you, Frankie. So much. More than anything."

"I love you, too," I whispered as he wrapped his arms around me. Here, in my childhood bedroom, I'd never felt more safe and sound.

THIRTY-THREE

Two weeks later, everything had changed.

After I released the video out into the world, I received plenty of supportive emails from friends and family. Most told me that they didn't intend to watch it, but I was brave for taking control over my life again in this way. Of course there were those whom I never heard from again; but they're not worth mentioning now. Most people were completely behind me, and they turned their wrath toward Piers. My story went around the globe, and I became a bit of a hero to those who'd been in similar situations. Turns out, there are a lot of us.

Thankfully, I never heard from Piers again. Without anything to hold over me, he disappeared into the wood-work. Supposedly, he lost his new job and was being investigated by the police, but by then, it didn't matter to me. He was a shadow of the man I'd known, but had I ever really known him? I think I was seeing what I wanted to see. I wanted the perfect life, but the perfect life is an illusion. The Piers Worthington I thought I was marrying was an illusion.

My father was back at work, back to his old self. Alex had come in, too, and had helped take the stress away—he'd always been better at these things than I was. I insisted on setting my dad up on a diet and—so far—he was being good about following it. He also didn't object to me hiring a chef to come in three times a week and prepare meals. Plus dad's assistant was under strict rules to make sure he didn't push himself too hard. Everyone at his company was thrilled by his return, and threw a party in his honour, where everyone assured me they'd be keeping a close eye on him. Turns out, my mum, Alex and I aren't his only family. That acknowledgement made me feel so much better, and like I wasn't abandoning him for Miami.

Of course, I had to return, if only to retrieve Saucy and the belongings I'd left behind. Michael had work to finish up out there too, so together, we boarded a flight back to the States.

As I sat down, I peered out the oval window, wondering what the future held. If I bounced around a little more before landing, fine. It didn't bother me, because for the first time, I felt like I'd be okay, no matter what. All I knew was that wherever I went and whatever I did, I'd be okay because I'd always have myself to fall back on. Knowing my worth gave me a surge of confidence and my heart swelled. As soon as Michael sat down, I grabbed his hand.

He studied me. "You don't like take-offs, either?"

I smiled as he leaned over and gave me a reassuring kiss on the forehead. "No. It's not that. I'm excited. For everything."

"Yeah?" His eyes darted over my face, confused. He was probably wondering why I looked so deliriously happy—because not all of it would be fun. I still had my termination with *Miami Scene* to figure out, and I didn't have a job. "Do you know what you're going to say when you meet with Gillian?"

I nodded and reached for my laptop. Yes, I was even giddy about that. "But I'm not going to *say* anything. I'm not going to meet with her. I'm going to do what I do best." Opening the lid, I powered it on. "I'm going to write the greatest article she's ever read, and she'll be begging me to come back."

Yes, I'd thought about it long and hard. I was going to write my entire story, everything, no-holds-barred. I was going to write about Piers, losing myself, nearly going off the deep end, flying to Miami, and finding myself again. I was going to cut open a vein and lay myself bare. I was ready, so much so that my fingers itched to pound the keyboard.

He laughed and squeezed my hand. "There's my girl."

That was it. I had my old spark back. I was that fearless girl again, the one who knew what she wanted, and went out, and took it.

As the plane set off, and I looked out at London, falling away beneath me, I knew I'd be back. Maybe not right away, but soon. Maybe I'd take trips to exotic locales like I used to, or stay home in bed and do absolutely nothing. Maybe I'd wear a bikini or even head to a nude beach or dance naked in public. Maybe Michael and I would get married and live an enviable, model life, or maybe we'd do some crazy things, like giving it up to move off-the-grid on an island in the South Pacific. There were no rules, there was only forward. It was *all* all right. Like Michael said, I could do anything I wanted to do. And I couldn't wait to start.

I looked at my screen and began to type. I wouldn't waste time sleeping on this flight, or any other flight, ever again.